STAKEOUT

The three lawmen wa[...]
watching from all a[...]
three cronies rode to [...]
their own mounts on [...]
dled stock in the corral between.

Longarm was hoping the four riders down below would move in closer. But then he saw Hoss MacLeod heave a resigned shrug and wheel his own mount the other way. As his followers moved to ride off with the son of a bitch, Longarm swung the muzzle of his saddle gun to train it their way as he called out, "That's far enough, MacLeod! Rein in and dismount and then grab for some sky if you ever hope to admire another sunset!"

DON'T MISS THESE
ALL-ACTION WESTERN SERIES
FROM THE BERKLEY PUBLISHING GROUP

THE GUNSMITH by J. R. Roberts
Clint Adams was a legend among lawmen, outlaws, and ladies.
They called him . . . the Gunsmith.

LONGARM by Tabor Evans
The popular long-running series about U.S. Deputy Marshal
Long—his life, his loves, his fight for justice.

SLOCUM by Jake Logan
Today's longest-running action Western. John Slocum rides
a deadly trail of hot blood and cold steel.

BUSHWHACKERS by B. J. Lanagan
An action-packed series by the creators of Longarm! The
rousing adventures of the most brutal gang of cutthroats ever
assembled—Quantrill's Raiders.

DIAMONDBACK by Guy Brewer
Dex Yancey is Diamondback, a southern gentleman turned
con man when his brother cheats him out of the family fortune. Ladies love him. Gamblers hate him. But nobody pulls
one over on Dex . . .

WILDGUN by Jack Hanson
Will Barlow's continuing search for his daughter, kidnapped
by the Blackfeet Indians who slaughtered the rest of his family.

LONGARM

AND THE LADY BANDIT

JOVE BOOKS, NEW YORK

This is a work of fiction. Names, characters, places, and incidents are either the product of the author's imagination or are used fictitiously, and any resemblance to actual persons, living or dead, business establishments, events, or locales is entirely coincidental.

LONGARM AND THE LADY BANDIT

A Jove Book / published by arrangement with the author

PRINTING HISTORY
Jove edition / May 2001

All rights reserved.
Copyright © 2001 by Penguin Putnam Inc.
This book, or parts thereof, may not be reproduced in any form without permission.
For information address: The Berkley Publishing Group,
a division of Penguin Putnam Inc.,
375 Hudson Street, New York, New York 10014.

The Penguin Putnam Inc. World Wide Web site address is
http://www.penguinputnam.com

ISBN: 0-515-13057-5

A JOVE BOOK®
Jove Books are published by The Berkley Publishing Group,
a division of Penguin Putnam Inc.,
375 Hudson Street, New York, New York 10014.
JOVE and the "J" design
are trademarks belonging to Penguin Putnam Inc.

PRINTED IN THE UNITED STATES OF AMERICA

10 9 8 7 6 5 4 3 2 1

Chapter 1

The State of Colorado fines you one hundred dollars for killing a porcupine with a gun, gives you a year of hard labor for deserting a herd of sheep in your charge, and hangs you by the neck until you are dead for stealing a horse.

Explaining how-come could be pure pleasure when the one who wants to know is a warm, sweet blonde with hair the color of taffy pulled by buttered hands, skin the tone of fresh-cranked vanilla ice cream, and big brown eyes the exact shade of hot chocolate on a crisp day.

Her given name was Alvina Lockwood and she'd asked U.S. Deputy Marshal Custis Long of the Denver District Court to join her in one of the Parthenon Saloon's private side-rooms when he'd sashayed in for some needed beer and the best free lunch within easy walking of the Federal Building on the Downtown Denver flats. Few men born of mortal women would have said no and Longarm, as he was better known in those parts, preferred the company of even a plain old gal to eating and drinking on his feet all alone at the bar.

The sweet warm blonde Longarm joined at the private marble-topped table with his beer schooner and plate of free lunch had been sipping her own mug of birch beer through a straw in the relative privacy you paid more for at the Parthenon. The gal was somewhere in her middle twenties with no baby fat to mention. But when he asked her how she felt about deviled eggs and pickled pigs' feet she shook her head almost wild enough to dislodge the straw boater pinned atop her upswept taffy tresses and demanded he tell her why they'd allowed some apparent lunatics to write the Criminal Code of Colorado. After she'd explained she was talking about such wildly disparate sentences for a gradually less cruel mistreatment of animals, Longarm washed down his chaw of cold cuts to soothingly reply, "Them sentences ain't meant to punish anybody for shooting a porcupine, deserting a herd of sheep, or stealing a horse, Miss Alvina. They are meant to discourage anyone in these parts from shooting a porcupine, deserting a herd of sheep, or stealing a horse. Before you bite my head off, I ain't trying to green you with Cattle Country Humor. The punishment for the abuses you just asked about are in proportion to the importance of the *critters* under the protection of the Colorado Criminal Code. As anyone can plainly see, a porcupine ain't worth a dollar, dead or alive. But it's about the only critter worth eating that a body lost in the high country without any bullets left could bring down with a club."

He made himself a rat-cheese and salami sandwich, with no bread, as he continued, "Porcupines and skunks are about the only fresh meat on the hoof that don't run too fast for a man on his feet with a club to catch and kill. Do I have to explain why most men would rather eat a porcupine? It ain't against the law to *kill* a porcupine for food, Miss Alvina. The state forbids anyone from *shooting* the same, see? Anybody lost in the woods with a gun and a few rounds of ammunition would rather

2

shoot a more appetizing critter for supper in the first place."

As he consumed his tidbit, having come to the Parthenon with grubbing up in mind, the birch-beer-sipping blonde across the table allowed she could see why they didn't want a shortage of porcupines over in the nearby Rockies. But, she demanded, wasn't a herd of sheep worth more in market value than your average saddle bronc?

Longarm swallowed, nodded, and explained, "Lots of greenhorns looking for a job out our way sign on for a summer of sheep herding without too great a grasp of how lonely and tedious the trade. Most any willing kid can be taught to keep a herd drifting safe across the high ranges above the timberline. The outfit he signs on with leaves him up yonder with plenty of supplies and at least two good sheepdogs to do most of the work. So they passed that law giving you a year at hard for just walking away from such a dull chore because a randy young cuss can get mighty itchy before he's relieved in the fall. Deserted sheep might manage to drift down to warmer pasture. They're more likely to just huddle together and run off a cliff, or die some other sheepish way. Sheep ain't exactly the smartest livestock to be found. But that one year at hard hanging over you for deserting the herd you were hired to take care of keeps most bored and lonesome young squirts on the job for at least one season."

"But how could *one horse* be worth even a small herd of grazing sheep?" she demanded in that reasonable patient tone women use when they want a man to demand a raise from the boss.

Longarm made a wry face and explained, "They were hanging men for stealing horses out our way before they ever got around to passing any laws protecting other critters. It ain't the dollar value of a horse that makes

3

its theft so serious, Miss Alvina. You can buy a scrub bronc for two dollars or less if you're willing to break it yourself. I could get you a well-trained cutting pony for under a hundred, down to the Diamond K on the Camp Weld Road, seeing you're a pal of mine. But there are times out our way when a man needs his horse so bad that you just can't put no dollar value on it. A man stranded on foot in the middle of an Indian Scare or say a blizzard clouding up above the Front Range can end up just plain done for. So, like I said, they don't hang you out our way for stealing horses. They hang you so that horses won't be stolen."

She stared soberly down at her birch beer, fluttering her lashes a mite, as she quietly murmured, "My poor brother, Edward, didn't know they could take a lark with another schoolboy's pony so seriously. You see, we both grew up in Ohio, where the authorities understand about silly college boys during spring break! Edward never rode off on that pretty palomino with any intent to *steal* it! He was only having fun!"

Longarm frowned thoughtfully as he shoved his beer schooner aside to soberly assure her, "As a federal lawman I have no jurisdiction if we're talking about college high jinks gone sour, Miss Alvina. But you might as well tell me about it. For I'll never get any sleep tonight unless I figure out what we're missing, here."

It only took her a few moments to tell her whole tale. It still made no sense to an experienced peace officer. For like most men who packed a badge, whether federal, state, or local, Longarm was expected to uphold the law and keep the peace, not to strive for needless trouble along with pointless litigation. So he told her, not unkindly, "Your brother or his lawyers have left something out, Miss Alvina. No offense, but his tale of woe, or a close version of the same, is not unfamiliar to my kind. Few if any horse thieves seem willing to confess to

4

grand larceny for fun or profit. That part about thinking
the pony you rode off with was a similar mount posessed
by a pal who might not have minded had you been able
to ask permission falls apart as soon as you fail to produce the pal with a matching pony."

She insisted her poor brother's fellow student owned
a palomino gelding just like the one Edward Lockwood
had ridden off with, but seemed to be unwilling to come
forward, lest he find himself in trouble as well.

Longarm was too polite to yawn at anyone that pretty.
But it wasn't easy to sound sincerely interested as he
soothed, "I'll ask some Denver copper badges I drink
with to let me have a look at their police blotter, Miss
Alvina. Are they holding your brother here in Denver
or up to the college town of Boulder where he . . . borrowed that palomino to ride in and enjoy the brighter
lights of a spring break?"

She said they were holding her poor brother in Denver
for a full-bore state trial, with a view to making an ex-
ample of him.

Longarm had to agree executing a college boy for
joyriding into the state capitol seemed a tad severe, but
explained, "The death penalty for horse thieves is an all
or nothing proposition, Miss Alvina. Once you start letting a horse thief off with five or ten at hard you lose
the magic of that more severe threat. They don't catch
one out of ten horse thieves to begin with. It's the ease
of getting away with the crime that makes it such a serious crime."

"Then there's no hope at all for poor Edward?" she
sobbed, those big brown eyes all warm and watery.

So Longarm caught himself saying, "I just told you it
was all or nothing, ma'am. They've either got to hang
him or drop the charges and let him off scot-free. So,
like I said, I'll ask for a look at their blotter and get back
to you as soon as I've a better handle on your brother's

5

fix. I have to report back to the federal building for some court duty this afternoon. I won't be able to drop by the local police headquarters before quitting time. So where do you reckon we might be able to get together this evening?"

She said she was staying at the Dexter Hotel a few streets over and allowed she might feel safe without an escort in her own lobby whilst she waited for him.

So they shook on it and Longarm headed back to work with a fist full of cold cuts and his poor gut still agrowl.

Reporting first to the office of his boss, Marshal Billy Vail, he asked young Henry, the clerk who played the typewriter and kept their files, if they had anything federal on one Edward Lockwood, a reputed newcomer to the owlhoot trail. When Henry just looked blank, Longarm explained how a frisky student off the nearby Boulder campus of the University of Colorado had been picked up in Denver aboard a palomino of some value, reported stolen a few hours earlier by its rightful owner. Longarm added, "Lots of old boys just starting out along the owlhoot trail never consider how easy it can be for the law to report their wicked ways by wire, most any direction they might ride."

Henry pursed his lips and said, "That hardly sounds like a federal case. Let Colorado hang the wayward youth. The only horse thieves we have on the front of our stove right now, if we knew who they were, would be the rascals who ran that remuda of cavalry mounts off that military range betwixt the South Platte and Camp Weld a few nights ago."

Longarm replied with a puzzled smile, "Somebody stole a whole bunch of army mounts and nobody thought to tell me, Henry?"

The clerk-typist sniffed and loftily replied, "There seemed no need to. You've been pulling court duty

6

down the hall and Marshal Vail said Deputies Gilfoyl and Keller both knew which end of a cavalry mount the horse apples fell from."

He added in a more comforting tone, "The trail was cold long before we got the complaint from the military police. As Marshal Vail remarked, with comments about a certain officer's ancestry, they'd have never in this world tried to saddle us with the case if they had any hope at all about those two dozen army bays."

Longarm grimaced and opined, "I follow old Billy's drift. It's tough to cut sign on a well-traveled postroad into town and they'd likely run the whole remuda into some seedy Denver livery corrals by the time the soldiers blue noticed the stock was missing."

He shrugged and added, "Those junior deputies are welcome to the exercise and I promised a lady I'd look into another charge of horse theft for her. I'll take your word her brother ain't in our federal files. That still don't let him off the hook by a long shot. All our serious horse thieves have to start out modest."

Having reported in, Longarm ambled down the marble hall to find the federal courtrooms at the far end still in recess. So he went looking for the fair but ferocious Judge Dickerson to see how much time he had left to kill.

He didn't find the white-haired lean and hungry-looking jurist in his chambers. He found the court stenographer assigned to the same case seated at His Honor's desk, filing her nails. As she glanced up to fix him with a radiant smile, Longarm ticked his hat brim to her and asked, "Might you know where the judge went, and when he might be back, Miss Bubbles?"

Miss Bubbles wasn't really the name the well-rounded, blue-eyed, and straw-blond little thing in well-stuffed polka-dot calico signed to the payroll, of course. They called her Miss Bubbles because nothing else described her half so well. Everything about her from her big blue eyes to her bee-stung lips and curvacious torso made her look as if she had been assembled, nicely, by a capricious Mother Nature playing with a big juicy bubble pipe. The temptingly put-together spheres of jigglesome flesh had been topped off by a mind, if you wanted to call it a mind, devoted to the pleasures of said flesh and a wicked sense of fun. He just knew that sooner or later she was going to get them both fired. For they'd once come close to getting caught in the act in that very room atop that very desk, and yet the tempting Miss Bubbles didn't seem to enjoy it off the premises after work.

So when she demurely replied, "His Honor was called over to the State House atop Capitol Hill and might not be back this afternoon. So he's asked me to hold the fort and tell anyone who asks that the trial of the soon-to-be-late Blake Prichard will resume tomorrow morn. So why don't you shut that silly door behind you and throw the bolt, you big tease? Have you been trying to avoid me, lately?"

To which Longarm could only honestly reply, "Yes, ma'am. Like I told you the last time in that file room down the hall, I'm too old to go back to herding cows for forty-and-found and you seem hell-bent on me getting caught at this job with my pants down! How come you never seem to want to meet me after work where we can take all the time we want in a nice soft bed at say the Tremont House or the Palace?"

Miss Bubbles looked insulted and demanded, "What kind of a girl do you take me for, Custis Long? You know what they call any woman willing to go up to a hotel room with a man she isn't married to, don't you?"

Longarm smiled wistfully and replied, "Yep, more sensible than sweet young things who prefer to be swept off their feet in broom closets or atop an office desk during business hours! Are you sure you don't get an added kick out of tempting fate that way, Miss Bubbles?"

She shrugged and rose behind the desk to unbutton her bodice as she giggled and jiggled, "I never came so hard in my born days as I did in these very chambers the afternoon we both heard the judge coming in!"

Longarm started to demand she cut that out. Then he shut the oaken door behind him and threw the bolt as he considered he'd soon have to behave himself with that sweeter and even warmer-looking blonde at the Dexter Hotel, after business hours.

Alvina Lockwood hadn't acted half as forward at the Parthenon and, even if she had, no lawman worth his salt was about to mess with a gal involved in a capital crime, even as a witness. So Longarm was able to assure himself, even as he unbuttoned his own tobacco tweed frock coat to get rid of his .44-40 and gunbelt, that he was only giving in, this one last time, for the sake of both young ladies.

Chapter 2

That old fuss who'd warned Prince Hamlet never to lie to himself had doubtless found his fool self atop a desk with somebody like Miss Bubbles. Nobody got through life without lying to themselves enough to keep from going crazy. But Longarm was honest enough with himself and enjoyed a good joke enough to suspect he'd have likely found some other excuse to screw Miss Bubbles if he hadn't been planning to meet a horse thief's sister after work. Miss Bubbles screwed like an alley cat in heat, and it was likely just as well they had to leave most of their duds on as she bumped and ground betwixt his gaping tweed fly and the green blotting paper atop Judge Dickerson's desk. For had they more time, and managed to do anything so grand stark naked, he'd have had a hell of a time getting over to the Dexter Hotel on his own two feet.

Once he'd had his wicked way with her bubblesome derriere atop the desk and his booted feet on the rug, Miss Bubbles shyly confessed she'd been saving another treat for him and suggested he haul down his tweed pants a mite more and have a seat in His Honor's swivel chair behind the desk. Longarm knew what she had in her alleged mind. He'd enjoyed one of her French lessons—a lot—in the past.

But even as he assumed the position behind the desk with his gunbelt across the blotter and Miss Bubbles out of sight under the desk, he had a time not asking why she enjoyed such crimes against nature. He knew a body blowing syncopated tunes on the French flute had a tough time trying to answer that question. If there was a sensible answer.

There was no doubt that Miss Bubbles was committing an offense against her own nature, as swell as it felt to him and as silly as he thought some of the state laws against the practice read. Longarm suspected that just as they hung horse thieves for stealing horses, they felt they had to throw cocksuckers in jail when they caught 'em because they caught so few and the practice seemed so widespread.

Yet he had to admit, as he leaned back in His Honor's scat to let her swallow as much of his turgid shaft as she desired, that the state laws they were violating seemed mighty picky, seeing that no serious harm was being done to anybody's person or property. It felt swell from his vantage point, and if she was getting some odd thrill from the pure perversity of her position on her knees under the desk, who's beeswax other than her own might it be?

He started to ask if she was fingering her ownself as she pleasured him with her pouty lips. Another gal he knew up to Sherman Street liked to diddle herself with a cucumber at such times, "To give my poor pussy a break," as she coyly put it. They'd told him down at the Silver Dollar about this rich mining man who paid the fancy gals extra to let him French their old ring-dang-doos whilst he jerked his fool self off with his hand. Some folk ate snails and fish eggs, too, after dining on all the steak and potatoes they'd ever wanted.

11

Longarm warned her he was fixing to come. But Miss Bubbles just sucked harder and seemed to be tuning a banjo under the skirts gathered up around her hips as, all of a sudden, there came a pounding on the door and a familiar voice rang out in no-nonsense tones, "Why is this door locked? What in thunder's going on in there?"

Longarm had been about to come but there was nothing like a bucket of ice water or a hanging judge pounding on a door secured with one measly bolt to cool a body down. So whilst it hadn't been easy, by the time the experienced Miss Bubbles had made it to the door to let the judge in, smoothed down and smiling innocent, Longarm was on his feet behind the desk with his fly buttoned fair enough and his gunbelt almost buckled.

Judge Dickerson was a hard man to convince. He asked how come the deputy assigned to the courtroom out yonder was at his desk, apparently arming himself against whatever they'd barred that door against.

Longarm allowed he'd been checking his chambers to make certain he had five in the wheel with the firing pin riding on a spent shell, in case that soon-to-be-late Blake Prichard's pals attempt to make good on them threats he made that morning. Then he asked how come His Honor had been over to the state house when he'd been fixing to invite Blake Prichard to a rope dance.

That worked. The judge sent Miss Bubbles to fetch some papers from the file room. But as soon as they were alone in his chambers, His Honor demanded, "Longarm, were you screwing that pea-brained blonde in here just now?"

Longarm soberly replied, "Your Honor, you have my word I wasn't *screwing* anybody in here, just now." And this was the simple truth, as soon as one studied on it.

Judge Dickerson knew Longarm hardly ever told a direct lie. So he shrugged and muttered, "I reckon she just can't win 'em all," and added, "They called me to

12

the statehouse for a meeting with the state and federal military men about that raid on the riding stock down to Camp Weld. I'm sure you understand how, since the war, the various state militias have been incorporated into a federally authorized National Guard?"

Longarm nodded and replied, "I was there, Your Honor. When that war betwixt the states broke out, the state militias of the succeeding states, commanded by their state governors, were organized as the Confederate Army, opposed to the Union Army made up of northern state militias along with the modest regular army, additional volunteers and, before it was over, cannon fodder drafted by both sides."

"You sound as if you don't approve of our struggle to preserve the Union, Deputy Long," the judge, who'd commanded a squadron of the 2nd Colorado in his day, remarked in a thoughtful tone.

Longarm shrugged and replied, with a clear conscience, "Most all of us approved the war when the first invites went out. But I'd as soon not talk about the way boys in blue and gray got to smelling under the peach trees of Georgia toward the end. Let's agree it made sense for Congress to semi-federalize the state troops after the war lest they ever be called out against the federal government again and get to how come everyone's so het up about those horses run off from Camp Weld."

His Honor said, "It was a mixed remuda of U.S. Cavalry and Colorado State Guard stock. So we've agreed to work together in the recovery capture phase, with the rascals who ran those military mounts off standing trial under the jurisdiction of Colorado, rather than the federal court those thieving sons of bitches were banking on!"

Longarm frowned thoughtfully and tried, "My boss, Marshal Vail, has said our court cases are jamming some

13

down to this end of the building, Your Honor."

Judge Dickerson snorted. "I can try a horse thief in half a day, and then I have to sentence him under our sissy federal statutes. Unlike my Colorado State colleagues, I'm not mandated to hang any son of a bitch of a horse thief!"

Longarm brightened as the penny dropped and said, "Now that you make mention of it, Your Honor, I did read something in the Police Gazette about Hanging Judge Parker, over to Fort Smith, sending Miss Belle Starr to a woman's reformatory for a bodaciously short time, considering how the charge had involved stolen horses. The reporters held Judge Parker might have been sweet on the ugly old bawd."

Judge Dickerson sniffed and flatly stated, "Poor Isaac threw the book at her and her Indian lover. The trouble was, and is, no federal court has the power to hand out more than a year at hard for a first offender convicted of stealing any livestock. Should they plead guilty, we have to let them off with an even lighter sentence, if you follow my drift."

Longarm did. He smiled thinly and said, "I can see why you'd as soon have us turn any horse thieves we catch with army mounts over to the tender mercies of a Colorado State court, Your Honor. I was just talking to a lady about a brother arrested as a horse thief. She says he only borrowed one pony, unauthorized, and faces a hanging. Yet, to hear you tell it, a smarter thief could steal a whole remuda of horses and get off with no more than a year on jail under federal law?"

Judge Dickerson smiled wolfishly and said, "One imagines that's why this bunch we're after has been stealing good military mounts rather than local range stock. They've hit other military ouposts along the foothills of the Front Range, north and south of here. I can hardly wait to see the expression on their faces when

14

they learn they're going to be tried on state rather than federal charges!"

Longarm nodded and agreed, "They'll likely feel chagrined, Your Honor. But what makes us suspect the same outfit of stealing military stock out our way of late? I just now heard that remuda from Camp Weld was run off by a party or partied unknown, with nobody witnessing the doubtless pre-dawn drive."

Judge Dickerson explained, "Nobody saw any of the military mounts in question being stolen. A sneak thief, by definition, steals things when nobody's looking. But after canvassing witnesses up and down the Front Range, more than once, the army provost marshal thinks he has a line on at least one member of the gang. Just before each raid, a young woman, a distinctive young woman on a pretty pony, was seen riding alone along the fence lines of the posts that have been raided. Doesn't it seem obvious she was scouting the lay of the land for the same gang?"

Longarm felt a big gray cat arch its back and swish its tail in his guts as he asked in a desperately calm tone, "Might this mystery woman scouting for the horse thieves be described as a warm honey blonde, Your Honor? I've a serious reason for asking!"

To Longarm's considerable relief, Judge Dickerson shook his head and said, "Redhead. Has strawberry braids and freckles from her chest up. Rides mannish, astride, in split buckskin skirts and a man's open workshirt. Tan sailcloth, open down the front a scandalous way for a she-male to ride, even on a warm day. She wears no hat. So there's no mistake about the hair and freckles. The few who've seen her on the trail described her as an easygoing country gal with a ready smile and a friendly wave, albeit inclined to keep her distance, as you'd expect a young gal riding alone. She's been spotted once in a blue shirt, but each and every time aboard that same strawberry roan that she must have picked to go with her hair. Nobody she passed, long before any stock was stolen, took her for anything worse than some gal visiting one of the spreads in their neck of the woods. The military police had to ask more than once before anyone who'd seen her put two and two together."

Longarm nodded thoughtfully and decided, "They'd be dumb to ride in with such a distinctive scout out on point. So we still don't know what any of the others might look like. But I would say that gal on the same roan has to be scouting for the same gang. Do you want me to talk to Marshal Vail about it or were you fixing to resume that trial out front this afternoon, Your Honor?"

The judge shook his head and said, "No to both questions. I understand Billy Vail and the provost marshal have plenty of men between them already working the case. I don't want to re-open the Prichard trial this late in the day. We have visitors from the east over at my place and I promised to get home early. But I will want you, and your six-gun, handy when I pronounce sentence on that murderous Blake Prichard, come tomorrow morn. So why don't you knock off early and get here on time in the morning for a change?"

Longarm allowed he did have some personal errands and asked in as light a manner as he could manage if it was possible for any horse thief to get out of hanging on that charge in Colorado.

Judge Dickerson shrugged and said, "Anything's possible. But a horse thief would have to eat cucumbers and perform other wonders to save his neck from your average judge and jury in *this* state. He'd have to turn State's Evidence against bigger fish at the very least. Maybe we'll be able to get the horse thieves we catch to lead us to that strawberry blonde scout. In case we don't round 'em up in a bunch."

16

Longarm hadn't been thinking about *those* horse thieves. But he thanked Judge Dickerson and they parted friendly enough.

Having more time to work with than he'd expected, Longarm made up for his skimpy noon meal at a chili parlor on Larimer Street and legged it on over to Police Headquarters.

He found his old pal, Sergeant Nolan, holding down the desk. So he was able to go through their books by a bright corner window whilst he smoked down two whole three-for-a-nickel cheroots and still wound up with the same discouraging results. So he thanked Sergeant Nolan and headed east to the Dexter Hotel well ahead of the time he'd told Alvina Lockwood to expect him.

As luck would have it, he knew the desk clerk of old from other occasions involving other ladies. So when his old pal told him Miss Alvina Lockwood was in, up in Room 303, Longarm allowed there was no call to announce the law ahead of time and just sashayed on up to the third floor on the sneak. He'd made more than one good arrest that way in his time.

But as he sort of hovered in the hallway outside Room 303, he didn't hear a thing going on inside. So, seeing she seemed to be really alone, he knocked.

The sweet warm blonde opened the door wearing nothing but her pongee kimono, with her taffy hair down, and that was just as well because the tawny pongee wasn't buttoned up the front.

She flustered, "Oh, Custis, I fear you've caught me fresh from my bath! I wasn't expecting you this early!"

Longarm stepped inside, lest somebody catch him jawing in broad day with a young lady that open to public view, and tried not to sound too stuffy as he told her, "I got off early. I just came from Denver P.D. and,

17

no offense, Miss Alvina, but somebody has been lying like a rug!"

She said, "I know! I just found out poor Edward seems to have met up with some dreadful people! But they just made a dreadful mistake! With Edward in jail, they seem to think I'm a horse thief, too! So might that not give us a grand chance to pull the wool over their eyes?"

Chapter 3

Longarm asked her to go first. But when she insisted he spell out his accusation he didn't want her to think he was holding back to trick her. So he perched on the windowsill to begin as she moved to a sideboard to build them some highballs.

He said, "The Denver P.D. and state prosecutor's office have a lot on you and your brother that you sort of left out, Miss Alvina. To begin with, it ain't your fault, but you're four years older than your brother, Edward, and he'd be a tad long in the tooth for a college boy if he was still enrolled as one, up Boulder way. But he flunked out a good five years ago and you've been supporting him and his drinking problem ever since."

She quietly turned to hand him a drinking problem of his own in the form of a heroic concoction of bourbon and branch water, calmly asking him, "How many people brag about a drunk in the family? It's true they chucked him out for taking more interest in wine, women, and song than he did in solid geometry and Latin verbs. But he really was at a frat party up in Boulder and he really thought the pony he borrowed to ride back to Denver belonged to another old grad who'd, ah,

19

shacked up for the weekend with . . . let's call her a co-ed."

Longarm shook his head and pointed out, "The University of Colorado ain't co-educational. But let's not worry about what some old pal might or might not have spent that weekend with. No lawman working for Denver or Boulder has been able to locate any of the parties your brother named when they arrested him in the company of that palomino. The lawsome owner of that expensive palomino is a real college boy with a generous allowance from a daddy in the cattle trade. Denver P.D. says he says he never heard of any Edward Lockwood. Nobody else at that frat party recalls the name, either, and the state prosecutor is banking on everybody sticking to that story and nobody dropping charges."

As she sat on the nearby bedstead with her own heroic highball, one bare knee peeked out at him from her loosely fastened kimono and he was suddenly aware of her lilac bath salts and how Judge Dickerson had cut things short as he'd been fixing to come, back at the federal building.

Shoving such thoughts aside, Longarm sternly went on, "Denver P.D. was a tad vague about your own exact address and visible means of support, Miss Alvina. I'd feel better about you supporting a weaker kid brother if you'd like to tell me how you manage that, dwelling in this transient hotel with no visible means of your own."

She sipped some inspiration, sighed, and said, "Neither my homespread nor mining and railroad stock portfolio are here in Denver. My late husband left me well provided for down by Pikes Peak. I oversee the operation of our stock spread now and again but spend more time at our town house in Manitou Springs."

Longarm sipped his own drink silently as he mulled that over. It sure beat all how a man could misjudge a well-preserved woman's age, even when she wasn't taking advantage of you with face paint and soft candlelight.

Misreading his silent admiration for more sinister suspicions, the surprisingly young-looking widow woman blurted, "Before you ask, there *was* a coroner's hearing and my husband's death was listed as perfectly natural. Despite what some might say down in Manitou Springs, I did not marry a rich old stockman for his fortune. Sidney had known my family back in Ohio before he came west after the war to earn that fortune on his own from scratch. He got in on the post-war boom out this way and the first time he married, thc trail-town tramp who trapped him *was* only after his money!"

Longarm made no comment. It was simply female nature to refer to all the women her man had ever slept with, save for herself, as tramps or worse.

The winner of that now-settled contest explained, "When he caught her with another man he settled some railroad stock on her and sent her and her beau on their way after she'd agreed to an uncontested divorce."

She smiled like Miss Mona Lisa and softly added, "The stock Sidney settled on them was overvalued paper he'd picked up for ten cents on the dollar to help an old friend, during the crash of '72. He and my dad had a chuckle about that when Sidney came east to attend a niece's wedding. He seemed pleased by the way I'd grown since he rode off to war with the Ohio volunteers and, well, we've all heard that story."

She sipped some more and mused, half to herself, "He wasn't that much older but a bullet he'd taken for the Union left him with weak lungs and we've all heard *that* story as well. I sent for Edward to join me out here when he graduated from high school to high jinks. I really thought he wanted to go to college. But we've been over that and poor Edward dosen't seem to have the makings of a cowboy, either. I haven't been able to keep him

21

down around Manitou Springs. He will divide his wasted time between the bright lights of Denver and the pontifications of a perennial sophomore."

"Sounds like an expensive way to manage," Longarm said dryly.

Her voice came through a tad slurred as she defiantly replied, "Have it your own way and let's say a weakling with a drinking problem got into bad company and did a dumb thing with a poor pony tethered on the street outside a drunken brawl. Can't we get him off by offering them some real full-time horse thieves?"

Longarm started to take another sip and decided not to. A man who packed a badge and a gun had to have a care about his other bad habits and he figured he was already at the stage where he was up to singing "John Brown's Body," a cappella, or laying lusty hands on most any sweet, warm taffy blonde he could get at.

He tried to modulate his response as he told her, "I asked you to go first with that brag about somebody mistaking you for another horse thief, Miss Alvina."

She nodded and said, "Downstairs, in the hotel dining room. He must have asked one of the help to point me out. I'd just come from meeting you at that dreadful place near your office, to partake of some coffee and cake at a corner table, when this dumpy little man with a bigger mustache than your own and a garish black and yellow Scotch plaid vest under his open buckskin jacket approached me."

"What kind of guns was he packing?" Longarm asked thoughtfully.

She stared up owlishly, refreshed her memory with another sip, and decided, "Two of them. Six-shooters with their ivory butts forward, the way you carry your own more modest revolver under that frock coat. He said his name was MacLeod, that he was sorry his old pal, Edward, had been picked up by the law, and that he still had the remuda he and Edward had been dickering about, if I was still in the market."

Longarm mulled that over, nodded, and decided, "The prisons of this land of opportunity are hardly crowded with college professors or civil engineers. A clever criminal is a contradiction in terms as soon as you study on it. So this horse trading MacLeod figured you might be in a sort of family trade with a known associate and then what?"

She finished her glass and rose, not too steadily, to move back to that sideboard as she explained, "I pretended not to have the slightest idea what he was talking about. I stalled for time by offering noncommittal answers until I understood he wanted to sell me a dozen well-bred bays, broken to more fashionable flat-saddles, with the smallest standing fifteen hands and all having Trakehner or Thoroughbred lines."

As she refilled her glass, Longarm murmured, half to himself, "In sum, the sort of stock the Army Remount Service pays top dollar for."

As she rejoined him by the cozy corner formed by the windowsill and bedstead, Alvina Lockwood demanded, "Did you think I didn't know that? I just told you I raised stock down by Pikes Peak. I've bought over-the-hill cavalry mounts for draft horses before this. When this loudly dressed Mister MacLeod said the stock he was offering had been freshly branded 808 I naturally knew they'd run the regular War Department US I was familiar with."

Longarm nodded soberly and agreed, "They usually settle on a new brand, changing that U to an O and the S to an 8. I've been trying to find a MacLeod in my mental file of wants out our way. He seems to have run that brand as well. While I'm still thinking along them lines, Miss Alvina, didn't you say both you and your kid brother were named Lockwood?"

She replied without hesitation, "Would you sign your married name to a hotel register if you were in town to bail out a horse thief and a lot of old biddies down in Manitou Springs still had you down as a gold digger who'd married a dying man for his money? It didn't occur to me until after he'd left that this mysterious Mister MacLeod hadn't made the connection because I was using my maiden name, making me appear a tad closer to my accused brother. Had I signed in as Mrs. Sidney Penn of the S Bar P, I doubt he'd have ever dared approach me with an offer of suspicious stock."

Longarm chuckled softly and decided, "That sounds reasonable. Keep going, ma'am. I like what I've heard so far."

She explained how, thinking fast on her feet, she'd stalled for time, wanting to see what sort of a deal she could make for her brother as she played the bigger fish on her line for suckers to be reeled in at her pleasure.

Longarm said, "I see more than one way to skin that cat, ma'am. If all else fails, I can ask this federal judge I know to transfer your brother to the Federal House of Detention as a material witness. But since all the lawmen on our side want to see them horse thieves hang for raiding Camp Weld and all them other military reserves, we ought to be able to get your kid brother off with a warning, if not a medal."

She tossed her empty glass aside and rose to kiss his cheek as she called him a darling man. Then, before Longarm could shift his grip on her to kiss her back right, she asked how he meant to capture the mysterious Mister MacLeod.

He hung on to her—she felt swell and smelled delicious—as he told her their best bet would be to round up all those stolen cavalry mounts along with anyone offering to sell them.

He explained, "It's just your word against his own if

24

I grab him down in the lobby or even up here as an announced admirer and, no offense, Denver P.D. has you down as the big sister of a suspected horse thief."

She snuggled more comfortably against him as she replied, with the bourbon, but no evidence of branch water, on her breath, "I could see that, even as I was sparring with the oily little man downstairs. So I said I needed time to hire a safe, secluded corral to look the stock over and bid for the same. I told him I knew a livery corral over by the Burlington Yards but needed time to withdraw some cash to work with tomorrow morning. I had no idea you'd show up so early. If I had, I'd have arranged the sale for this evening. The shady Mister MacLeod was unbudging on that one point. He said it had to be this evening or, if not, tomorrow evening, around quitting time, with the streets crowded and the dust stirred high in the tricky gloaming light around sundown, if Edward and me really wanted those fine saddle mounts."

Longarm nodded and muttered, "Sounds as if he's traded in stolen stock before. Witnesses recall stock passing, day or night, when things are calm and quiet. Late tomorrow gives us plenty of time to cut a deal with the powers that be and stake out that corral you just mentioned. How are you supposed to get word to this MacLeod jasper once you've drawn some cash and stand ready to bid on them ponies?"

She said, "I asked about that. He said there's no need for us to get together again until and unless I'm ready to deal. He said he and his hands would run that 808 remuda to the corral I'd mentioned along about suppertime. I asked what he meant to do if they didn't find me waiting for them there. He just laughed and said, in that case, what he might or might not do next was nothing for me to worry my pretty little head about. I think he was sort of flirting with me."

Longarm said that sounded reasonable and kissed her right. She kissed back in a manner assuring him she'd been married up, some, and enjoyed it whilst it had lasted. But it was still broad day outside and a man ate an apple a bite at a time. So he stopped kissing her, but hung on to her some, as he said, "Unless your flirty Mister MacLeod has somebody watching you, he's got something dirtier in mind. A man would have to be a total fool to approach a strange gal with such an offer and then agree to meet her with the stolen goods on pure speculation."

She said, "Well, he has me down as a horse thief's sister and I did say I'd get some money at the bank. I naturally have a business acount at Drover's Trust under my married name. We ship from here in Denver."

Longarm nodded but said, "I don't want you going near that Drover's Trust. MacLeod or some other crook could ask about you at your bank as easily as they could ask about you at your hotel."

She noticed that he seemed to be seating her back on the bedstead and she coyly suggested, "We don't have to go out at all, until you're ready to arrest the brute. Room service will send up most anything we might feel the need for as we . . . pass the time."

Longarm was glad he'd stopped drinking when he had. It was still a chore, keeping his wits about him, as she reclined back on one elbow to let her kimono open wider. He said, "We don't have as much time as you might think, Miss Alvina. I have some federal and state judges to talk to. Then I have to get my boss, Marshal Vail, to let me gather a whole heap of deputies and fill them in on the plan. We'd best let Denver P.D. in on the roundup if we expect them to be more understanding about your kid brother. You'd better give me the location of that secluded corral before I leave."

She protested, "I don't want you to leave! What am

I supposed to do with myself, waiting so long, all alone up here?"

He soothed, "I'm sure you'll think of something, ma'am. It's best if we see as little as possible of one another until we're ready to move in on the rascals. I don't want to brag, but I am not known anywhere in Downtown Denver as a likely horse thief. Should anyone ask, before I can get back to you, tell them the truth, sort of. Say it's true you were asked a lot of pesky questions about your kid brother by a U.S. deputy marshal. That ought to hold 'em."

He got out his notebook and repeated his request for the location of that planned horse trade with the mysterious MacLeod.

She gave it to him. He knew the area near the south end of the railroad yards. Then she blurted, "Can't you come back later tonight, after dark when nobody need know? I'm scared, Custis. Scared and lonesome and suddenly hungry for feelings I'd almost forgotten until you kissed me, just now!"

Longarm smiled down wistfully and replied, "I'm in worse shape, then. I knew what I wanted before I ever kissed you. But we'd better worry about our feelings later, after we've settled this other business and don't have any *other* worries in our way, say tomorrow night?"

She made a withering remark about his manhood and he got out of there before he was tempted to whip it out and prove her wrong. For a lawman who acted that free with his old organ grinder would have to be as dumb as a horse thief who trusted strange gals on no more than their smiles and eyelash flutters, for Gawd's sake!

Chapter 4

The sun was still distressingly high as Longarm left the Dexter. So there he was on the sunny streets of Downtown Denver with a hell of a hard-on and no place to put it until he tended to some chores as long as he still had the time.

Back at the federal building, he found his boss, the somewhat older and way shorter and fatter Marshal Billy Vail, was pleased as punch to hear Longarm had a line on those sons of bitches who'd raided Camp Weld. He said he'd heard rumors about a horse trader they called Hoss MacLeod, but, to date, nobody had been able to pin anything on the fast-talking Scotchman. On those few occasions he'd been caught trying to sell a purloined pony MacLeod had, so far, been able to produce bills of sale and plausible stories. Gents who ran hock shops in cow country were seldom arrested if they had any explanation at all for that dead posse rider's saddle gun in their window, either. You had to catch a receiver of stolen property in the act.

Vail offered Longarm one of his stinky cigars and even a seat in his oak-paneled office as they decided on the corporal's squad of gun hands Longarm wanted for the stakeout. Longarm didn't have to tell an old man hunter who'd broken in as a pre-war Texas ranger how more than six or eight men tended to cross-fire into one another during a shoot-out. But when Longarm suggested they move Edward Lockwood to a safer cell in their own house of detention, Vail shook his bullet head and said, "You and me betwixt us don't have the authority and, should we try, and fail to take him away from Colorado, we'd be risking them outlaws noticing we might be on to something. It's best to leave sleeping dogs and arrested horse thieves lie until we can get a court order from Judge Dickerson down the hall."

Longarm said, "I understand His Honor planned on leaving early this afternoon, Boss."

Vail nodded and replied, "You heard right. But I understand his court stenographer, that one they call Miss Bubbles, might still be on the premises if you have any unfinished business with her boss."

Longarm dryly remarked any unfinished business with her boss could wait and got out of there as soon as he could get Henry to type up and post the duty roster where the others he'd selected would see it in the morning. Then he left before Miss Bubbles found out he was back in the federal building. A man, however strong, had to know his own weaknesses, and how many times in one afternoon was a poor boy with a hammering hard-on supposed to turn down temptation?

He didn't want to avoid Miss Bubbles because he didn't want another go at her. He wanted a go at *somebody* bad enough to taste it. But a man with chores to tend to could put off pausing for a set-down meal, some slap and tickle, or even a serious shit until he has some damned free time.

On the face of it, he had plenty. That was why he meant to make the most of the better than twenty-four hours Alvira Lockwood had given him to work with, if she'd been on the level. But he headed next for the county jail to see if he could make certain she'd been on the level.

They let him jaw with Edward Lockwood alone in an interrogation room, seated across a zinc-topped table from one another with plenty of coffee and ashtrays to work with.

Edward Lockwood was a pasty-faced cuss with a drinker's nose who looked a tad old for frat parties. He barely worked as Alvira's kid brother until you considered what hard liquor and flabby willpower could do to anybody. He seemed suprised to learn his big sister had come up from Manitou Springs and gone to bat for him. He said Alvina had been mighty mean when he'd been sent home from college, dead-drunk in a hired carriage, but admitted she'd bailed him out more than once when he'd wound up flat broke in the Denver drunk-tank, facing thirty days or thirty dollars, payable to the court in cash or hard labor.

Longarm lit the weak-chinned wastrel's cheroot for him, seeing Lockwood's hand were shaking so, as he said, firmly but not unkindly, "Your sister seems to have more use for you than we do, unless you'd care to cut this bullshit about borrowed palominos and talk about Hoss MacLeod."

Lockwood blinked in surprise and asked, "Who told you about him?"

Longarm shook out the match head as he calmly replied, "He told us about himself. He seems to think your sister, Miss Alvina, has been stealing or dealing in stolen stock, her ownself."

Lockwood laughed, wild-eyed, and protested, "Jesus H. Christ, Alvina is a member of the Women's Christian Temperance Union, down in Manitou Springs!"

Longarm glanced away with a sort of Mona Lisa smile of his own and confided, "Ladies who don't ap-

30

prove of strong spirits have been known to indulge in other vices. Suffice it to say your pal, Hoss MacLeod, has offered to sell her a whole heap of saddle stock with fresh-run 808 brands. So what can you tell us about them recent raids on our military reservations, and it sure would help if you could name that strawberry blonde on a strawberry roan they have scouting ahead for 'em?"

It didn't work. Lockwood admitted he not only knew Hoss MacLeod, but might have sold him some stray ponies he'd sort of stumbled over out on the range. But after that he swore he didn't know toad squat about any cavalry mounts or that mysterious freckle-faced rider. He said the only gal he'd seen in Hoss MacLeod's company had been Mex, albeit not bad.

Longarm decided he'd told the contrary cuss more than he should have and took the time and another cheroot to spin him a tangled web meant to confuse the shit out of Lockwood and any crooks coming to visit him, as say, a lawyer really working for Hoss MacLeod. He left Alvina's kid brother, he hoped, with the notion that Alvina hadn't told him a whole lot when he'd gone to the Dexter to question her.

Then, out at the front desk, he made sure they'd let him know when and if Lockwood had any such visitors. They, in turn, assured Longarm nobody, not even his sister, had been by since he'd been sent over from his booking at Police Headquarters.

By this time the sun was closer to the darkening peaks of the Front Range, over to the west. So, having done all he could for the moment, Longarm allowed it was about time he did something about that hard-on.

He had to eat supper first with another young widow woman up atop Capitol Hill in a fancy Sherman Street brownstone. The sacrifice wasn't all that painsome as they dined alone on fancy French grub served on Sterling silver atop Irish linen with her hired help running back and forth from the kitchen. His voluptuous hostess told him the tasty flapjacks they had for dessert were called Crappy Suzies. But they tasted fine, and as the help cleared the table, the young widow woman told them to just leave the dishes in the sink and take the rest of the evening off.

She was already unpinning her soft brown hair in the front parlor by the time she covered an unconvincing yawn and said something about feeling so tuckered after a long day supervising the production of all those Crappy Suzies.

So Longarm allowed he was bone weary as well and they went on up to her quarters to prove they'd both been fibbing about how much they both needed some sleep. She didn't even let him stretch out on the four poster beside her until he'd shoved it to her three times in a row, in more than three positions and, even then, she insisted on getting on top as he lay spread-eagle and jay naked across the rumpled bedding with a lit cheroot gripped in his grinning teeth.

Longarm didn't mind. For a gal who handn't had to work since her own rich husband had left her so much free time, she rode a heap and had enough strength in her shapely thighs to move all those hourglass curves and bounding breasts with the glee of a mean little kid going up and down on a merry-go-round.

But of course, being a woman, as soon as she'd satisfied herself by abusing him like a painted pony, she naturally started to cuss him out for not having been by in a coon's age.

When he told her he'd been on court duty since coming in from the field mission they'd talked about, the last time, she flopped down at his side to steal his cheroot as she said, "Pooh, you men are all alike and I'll bet you only came by tonight because some younger girl you've been messing with refused you!"

As she took a drag on his smoke, Longarm assured her, truthfully, as soon as you studied on it, "As a matter of fact I had my choice of two willing women this afternoon. But do you see me anywhere but here with you?"

She handed back the cheroot and snuggled closer as she demurely asked whether either of those other ladies had hare lips or triple titties.

He smiled at the picture and once more honestly replied, "A gal with three tits might have tempted me. I'll tell you true I was tempted by the two I just mentioned. Have you ever heard tell of another widow woman named Lockwood, I mean Penn, down to Manitou Springs?"

The Denver socialite looked surprised and asked, "Alvina Penn, owns and operates the S Bar P? How on earth did you ever meet that queen of all snobs, you poor dear?"

Longarm took a drag on the cheroot and replied, "It's a gift I have, I reckon. Her kid brother is in a mess and I reckon she felt she might catch more flies with honey than with vinegar. Her brother said she was a member of the W.C.T.U. and can I take it she's rich enough to get away with such airs?"

The widow woman, who was rich enough in her own right, began to toy with his limp virility as if to make certain it was still under her control as she made a wry face and replied, "Stinking rich, thanks to a husband with the morals of an Arabian rug merchant and the honesty of a riverboat card shark. Played the Indians against one another down in the South Park during that big running gunfight between the Arapaho and Ute. Wound up with water rights few other white men knew about just as they were starting to strike color and sprout hungry mining towns down that way. But tell me about the mess her brother is in, Custis. I didn't know she had anyone out our way to worry about. From what I hear, she's never worried much about anyone but her own snooty self!"

Longarm said, "Reckon there are some kid brothers nobody wants to brag about."

Then, seeing she'd taken to stroking with some skill, he snuffed the cheroot to return the favor and they forgot all about Alvina Penn and her own problems as they worked to solve a more interesting one his gracious hostess had read about in the Kama Sutra, that illustrated and mighty troublesome Hindu treatise on sexual contortions.

It was easy enough to convince her, once they'd tried, how impossible it was for him to get it in if they both tried to cross their ankles behind their own necks. He couldn't manage that position with nobody in the way. But it was fun, for a few strokes, once she'd manged with two pillows under her shapely rump, with him on top on braced knees and locked elbows as she guided his questing shaft where they both wanted it.

But of course, in the end, as ever, they wound up swapping spit and just bumping and grinding the old-fashioned way to finish right. So when she commenced to cry as they clung limply satisfied in one another's arms, Longarm soothed, "Don't be too disappointed, Lamb Chop. I warned you the Hindu artist who drew those sassy pictures had more imagination than direct experience with human anatomy. I've always suspected that French pornographer, De Sade, hadn't been getting any when he wrote that dirty book about Miss Justine. Pimple-faced kids swapping brags in pool halls tell amazing tales of Slap-and-Tickle, too."

She sniffed and murmured, "Girls showing off with their fingers make up silly stories, too. You didn't disappoint me, darling. As ever, you thrilled me from my curled under toes to the very roots of the hair on my

34

head. Nobody has ever made me come so passionately and that makes me so mad!"

Longarm didn't answer. Any man who said anything when a woman got to talking like that snuggled bareass against him was a man who'd been behind the door when the brains were being passed out!

Since the ball was still in her court, she felt she had to explain, "We've always been honest with one another, Custis. We both know you've been with other women and I've never tried to tell you that you were the only man I've ever slept with since my poor husband was taken from me by a cruel fate."

Longarm had no answer for that, either. So she went on, "Of all the men I've ever made love with, including, alas, my late husband, I have never had anything inside me as grand as that thing you describe so well as your old organ grinder. So I just can't get enough of it and there's just no way you can give me half as much as I want!"

Longarm cautiously tried, "We've talked about my job and some of the funerals I've had to attend. But look on the bright side. Even if we could marry up, consider how awful it might feel if ever we got all we wanted of one another and got to picking at one another's way less appealing points!"

She kissed his bare shoulder and sighed, "I wouldn't care if you went fat and bald on me as long as I could have your best feature all to myself every night. But we both know how impossible that would be, don't we, darling?"

Longarm managed not to sound relieved as he asked, "We do?"

She kissed him some more and insisted, "I can't even have you visit me like this as often as I'd like, lest the neighbors gossip about me even more. And of course, marriage between a working class lawman and a woman

35

of my position would be simply impossible!"

So once she began to bawl some more about that Longarm took her in his arms to comfort her some more and with one thing leading to another they wound up in the rug with him on top as she marveled at his endurance.

So he didn't tell her how he was using Miss Bubbles and Alvina Penn, in turn, as added inspiration as he discharged his repeating weapon in the same old pal again.

Picturing the teasing Miss Bubbles totally bare and willing to go at it old-fashioned in private was inspiring enough. But now that he felt Alvina Penn was most likely safer to screw than he'd thought, he sure wanted to have her in this very same position and, Lord have mercy if he hadn't almost called this other young widow woman Alvina as he was coming in her!

Chapter 5

It was just as well they'd gone to bed right after supper because, as ever, his gracious hostess atop Capitol Hill ordered him out of the house before dawn lest anyone but the alley cats comment on a grown man slipping out the back door of a respectable widow woman.

So he got an unusually early start on the day. But nobody at the office commented on that, because his on-and-off affair with the widow woman on Sherman Street wasn't as big a secret as they liked to think.

Thanks to his early start, Longarm had things all set to go before noon and hired yet another hotel room at the nearby Tremont House before he sent one of the homelier stenographers from the federal building to the Dexter Hotel with a message for that sweet, warm taffy blonde.

Alvina Lockwood Penn showed up at the Tremont House within the hour, looking confused, even before Longarm popped out from behind some lobby rubber plants to whisk her up a back stairwell and along a deserted hallway to the sunny corner room he'd hired.

As he shut and bolted the door behind them, Alvina

gasped, "How did you know? Oh, Custis, I've so much to tell you!"

He waved her to a seat on his own hired bedstead and moved over to a dresser to build the highballs, this time, with Maryland rye and ice water from the hotel kitchen as she went on, "That MacLeod person sent word to me at the Dexter. He said they'd been watching from across the street. I told that girl you sent about that and she said you'd already thought of that and wanted me to leave by their alley exit. How did you know they might be watching that other hotel, Custis?"

"Lucky guess." He replied as he turned to her with the highballs. She was now fully armored in a summer-weight blue gingham frock and yet another straw boater with a stuffed hummingbird perched atop it and, worse yet, that bodice was thin and snug enough to reveal the edges of the infernal corset she was wearing under it.

But they had plenty of time to worry about that. So he sat on the bedstead beside her to hand her one tall glass as he explained, "It ain't that we get that much *smarter* as we grow older. I doubt I could beat my twenty-year-old self too bad at checkers. But we do get *wiser* as we circle through life on the same old merry-go-round. So I *know* a heap more than my twenty-year-old self and I've heard of crooks watching from across the way before. That's why I asked you not to leave the Dexter for any reason before you heard from me, see?"

She placed her untasted drink on a nearby windowsill, saying she was so ashamed about getting tipsy on him the day before. Then she told him, "They wanted to know about that. The young lady they sent to see me at the Dexter said her boss was concerned I hadn't gone to the bank as I promised. I told her I'd sent somebody, lest somebody else, such as a lawman like you, wonder why I might be drawing cash from my account. She said her boss had asked at the bank and they'd said nobody named Lockwood banked there. So you were right about them not knowing much about me, save that I was kin to poor Edward. I think I fooled them by just laughing and pointing out how dumb it would be for her Mister MacLeod to sign his real name to anything."

Longarm smiled and said, "There you go, I told you we got wiser as we got older. Tell me more about this gal they sent to ask about your bank account. Might she by any chance have been a redhead or at least a strawberry blonde?"

The tawny blonde Alvina made a wry face and decided, "I suspect sun bleached, if not bottle bleached carrot top and freckles. Irish as Paddy's pig, dressed in a cheap new dress with the price tag still in place on the hem. She walks like a farm girl, too."

Longarm nodded and said, "Other witnesses have only seen her in the saddle. We're after the right bunch, sure as shooting, and when I spoke to Judge Dickerson about your brother this morning he told me Edward will be listed as a federal witness so's we can get him out of that county jail, but never called to testify, lest he testify for the other side. His Honor figures we'll have enough for a conviction, in a state court on a capital charge, once our combined state and federal trap is sprung on Hoss MacLeod and those incriminating cavalry mounts. How come you've suddenly rejoined the W.C.T.U. Miss Alvina? Wasn't it your own grand notion to pour *me* a drink, just yesterday?"

"I was trying to seduce you," she quietly confessed, looking away from him with a becoming blush to her cheeks as she added, "I was desperate. They told me they were going to hang my poor weak brother! How was I to know you'd be so understanding and so nice?"

Longarm swallowed a good stiff belt of watered rye. Then he smiled and sheepishly decided, "That kindly old philosopher who first opined, no doubt in French, that

39

nice boys go home from the dance alone, must have noticed how much you ladies enjoy taming beasts, for all your complaints about beastly menfolk. But getting back to other nice kids, did that cowgirl they sent to see you mention any change of plans for later this evening?"

Alvina shook her head and replied, "Only a few added details. I guess that MacLeod person has had more time to think since our first meeting. He said I can bring some wranglers of my own, but none of us are to show up before sundown. He says he'll have somebody watching that out-of-the-way corral I suggested and that the deal will be off unless we do things his way, to the letter."

Longarm reached under his coat for the survey map he'd brought over from the federal building as he nodded and said, "Then we'd best do it his way to the letter."

He moved his hips further from her own to spread the ink on onion skin, tracing on the bedding between them, asking if she read maps. A younger lawman might not have noticed how many witnesses there were in his world who couldn't read anything.

She said she ran a stock spread and held water rights in the South Park, for heaven's sake. So Longarm placed a fingertip on the crispy thin paper to say, "Bueno, here's your Kiowa Livery, near that angle where 24th Street hooks into Wazee Street near the Burlington Yards. So here's their combined corral and shipping chutes betwixt Wazee and the freight sidings. Have you the least notion where they might have that stolen military stock, right now?"

She said, "Of course not. They never told me. That MacLeod person said, and that redhead repeated, that they meant to shift the remuda through the maze of chutes and pens alongside the railroad yards near sundown, in the confusion of quitting time and some freight trains due to load stock for cooler night runs. That girl

40

said they'd be watching behind the Kiowa Livery and that once they were sure it was safe they'd run those fine cavalry bays into that corral, where Mister MacLeod would meet me, alone, with his own help covering us from a safe distance with rifle guns. She said that her boss had bad feelings about the way our deal was going and not to wait for him if there was nobody there this evening. What could I have done to make him so uneasy, Custis?"

Longarm left the map spread open between their hips as he quietly replied, "Some of us men find sudden changes of mood unsettling, Miss Alvina. It's as likely that, like that other gal said, Hoss MacLeod has had time to study on how well he really knows you and your brother. I got Edward to own up to knowing Hoss MacLeod when I spoke with him, by the way. So if your brother was telling the truth about only selling a stray pony to Hoss now and again, I can see how Hoss might feel itchy about a Lockwood he knows even less about, no offense. They told me at the office that Hoss MacLeod has managed his somewhat shady horse swaps without ever being caught red-handed. I'm commencing to see why. There has to be a better way."

She smiled uncertainly at him to volunteer, "I don't see how we can fail, if he shows up with those stolen horses at all. You and your own followers will be covering me as I ride in, alone, to meet with this Hoss MacLeod as we agreed, right?"

Longarm shook his head and said, "Wrong. That's too big a boo by half. MacLeod and his gang are already on the prod and, try as I may, I can't come up with any sure way to avoid gunplay for certain. So I reckon we're going to have to work with what we have and hope for the best."

He had another look at his map, and began to fold it back up as he continued, "I learned in this war they gave

41

one time not to use the highest steeple overlooking the field of fire for an observation post. The enemy always suspects and shells such high points. But on the other hand, you can see for city blocks in all directions from the loft of an average warehouse or a third-story office window. But before I figure where to set up my own gun hands, here's what I want you to do."

She seemed to be listening. So he told her, "I want you to stay put, right here, whilst I arrange to get your baggage from that other hotel and hire you a private compartment on a southbound Pullman train leaving just this side of three this afternoon. Then I want you to go on home to Manitou Springs and just sit tight until your brother, Edward, can join you. Judge Dickerson promised me your brother will go free as soon as we recover them ponies and have the others locked up."

She protested, "Pooh, you're no fun! I want to help you catch those awful crooks who led poor Edward down the Primrose Path!"

Longarm dryly replied, "Drunks find their own way to the Primrose Path. But a deal is a deal and I told you he gets off when they get caught. Meanwhile, you're too young to die and too pretty to get all scarred up with shotgun pellets. So, like the Indian chief said, I have spoken."

He finished his drink, stood up, and asked if he could order her anything from room service on his way out. She shot a thoughtful look at the Maryland Rye and pitcher of ice water on the dresser and told him she could go for some sandwiches.

He sent a bellhop up with some ham and cheese on rye to go with any Maryland Rye she felt up to whilst the W.C.T.U. wasn't looking.

He didn't consider her two-faced. Recalling how she'd put her booze away the day before. Not deliberately two-faced, least ways. Having packed a badge for

42

six or eight years, Longarm had learned most all of us were inclined to be of more than one mind about a heap of things. Half the Mex gals he'd ever spent the night with had crosses above their beds or plaster saints watching from a nearby shelf. He was sure more than one of them had gone to Confession to brag about him, later. He knew a heap of society gals joined the Women's Christian Temperance Union for the tea, cake, and gossip gatherings they gave, whether they enjoyed a little wine with their dinners or not. Nobody managed to be all out good or all out bad, all the time. They said Frank and Jesse were devoted to their mother and hadn't that famous preacher run off with a choir lady that time?

Knowing Hoss MacLeod had declared himself right proddy about the next few hours, Longarm took extra care and sent other deputies to check Alvina out of the Dexter and book her that private compartment for later that afternoon. Having assured the gal's safety, he was back to worrying about the harder parts by the time he ambled back to the Tremont House, around one-thirty.

He'd told her to bolt the door after him and not to open for anyone but himself or room service. So he was a tad surprised when he tapped softly and she replied, from the other side, that the door was open.

So he opened it and went on in with a puzzled frown to find the sweet, warm taffy blonde in bed, under just one sheet, with her summer frock and corset over the brass footrails and her hat on the dresser, near what was left of the ice water and Maryland Rye.

She smiled up at him, sort of owl-eyed, to say, "Oh, Custis, I feel so silly!"

He had to laugh as he bolted the door behind him and got rid of his own hat and coat, saying, "You look silly, too. It's after one and you've a train to catch a little after three, Miss Alvina!"

43

She giggled, burped, and suggested, "In that case, don't you think we'd better hurry?"

Noting his hesitation, the taffy blonde frowned up at him to demand, "What's the matter? Don't you want me?" as she tossed the sheet aside to reveal all she had to offer, stark naked, save for her black lisle stockings, gartered just above her shapely knees. He couldn't help noticing she was taffy blonde all over.

So he sighed and said, "Well, sure I want you. Do you take me for a wooden Indian? But, like I said, we ain't got much time and, well, to tell the truth, I don't shoot sitting ducks or steal pennies from blind news dealers, either."

She nodded in sudden understanding and replied in a more sober tone, "Oh, for heaven's sake, I'm not really that drunk, you big goof. I just thought you'd feel more . . . forward, if you thought I'd indulged a bit. Would you feel more comfortable if I simply suggested it might be nice to fuck, as long as we had the time to kill?"

Longarm laughed like hell and moved to the dresser to pour himself a stiff one, and to hell with the ice water, as he suggested, "Make more sense if we took the time to do it right, say down in Manitou Springs when I deliver your baby brother to you safe and well?"

She sighed and pulled the sheet back over some of her, saying, "You know I belong to the W.C.T.U. in Manitou Springs and you can shoot a rifle ball the length of Grand Avenue without hitting anybody who'd approve of us tearing any off down yonder!"

He sighed, swallowed his bracing drink, and soothed, "In that case we'll have to make certain nobody from the W.C.T.U. is watching, Miss Alvina."

She protested, "Damn it, I want to fuck here and now. For I'll never be able to fuck you if Hoss MacLeod kills you this evening and *then* what can we do?"

44

He poured another shot as he replied, "You'll still be able to work something out with somebody or something else. I won't have to worry about doing nothing if they kill me and I follow your drift entire. But I'm too weak willed to take you up on your kind offer, ma'am."

She propped herself up on one elbow, allowing the sheet to fall away from her turgid nipples again as she demanded in a confused tone if he'd been paying any attention to his own words.

She said, "Correct me if I'm wrong. But did you just imply you felt too uncertain of your willpower to just give in and get out of that ridiculous vertical position?"

He nodded soberly and said, "I told you you have a train to catch. If I'm to see you safe aboard it we have to leave this hotel room no later than quarter-to-three if we go by hansom cab. So what kind of a sissy would I have to be if we expected me to screw you as sincerely as I'd like to screw you in just one lousy hour?"

She smiled up at him, radiantly, and agreed that, since he put it that way, all was forgiven until she could get him alone again behind her bedroom door down in Manitou Springs.

Chapter 6

Longarm saw the fully dressed but sweet, warm taffy blonde off at the Union Station with Maryland Rye on both their breaths as they took time out for a long lingering kiss, of the French variety.

That left him plenty of time to set up his stakeout around the Kiowa Livery betwixt Wazee Street and the confusion of dusty sun-silvered corral rails to the west. Most of the small-to-medium-sized holding pens were empty. Others were crowded with bawling cattle, sheep, and, of course, some ponies. Longarm figured it would be risking too much to scout about for those missing military mounts ahead of time. There were too many places to hide a horse in that part of town and the gang would be on the alert for such a move.

Longarm had taken up his own position in the hayloft above the livery stable fronting on Wazee, with his field of fire out the back, across the corrals and railroad yards beyond. It was now pushing five in the afternoon and he was up there with two junior deputies they called Smiley and Dutch. Smiley was the family name of the otherwise morose Pawnee breed who seldom spoke and never seemed to smile. Nobody could pronounce the outlandish High Dutch name of the shorter and more happy-looking natural born killer they usually teamed with the more steady Smiley. They made a good team. Smiley tended to study some before he drew on a suspect. Dutch was inclined to draw and fire in about the time Smiley could decide they might be in trouble.

It was naturally the more trigger-happy Dutch who kept asking Longarm what time it was and what in thunder might have gone wrong.

To which Longarm could only reply, more than once, "Hold your horses and, once they get here, hold your fire! I mean that, Dutch. We want to take at least one member of the gang and all those stolen horses alive!"

"There ain't nobody coming." Dutch pouted, like a kid weary of waiting for Christmas or his birthday.

Longarm was as anxious, knowing he'd be blamed if the deal fell through and just as tired of sprawling in all this dessicated hay in a tweed outfit too warm by half for such a warm and lazy afternoon. It didn't make him feel any better to picture himself undressed back at the Tremont House with a slightly tipsy and mighty willing widow woman.

A million years later a factory whistle moaned in the distance and somewhere closer they heard gals laughing their way out some doorway to head on home, unless they had better places to go.

Longarm idly wondered whether Miss Bubbles and that new darker gal who'd come to work at the federal building were giggling their way down the stone steps, anxious for some action after an honest day's work.

But nothing happened for another million years as the sun sank ever lower with wagon wheels and clopping hoofs stirring up a haze of fine dry dust to blur things over to the west still more as the setting sun shone in their eyes.

Then the usually silent Smiley, possessed of Indian

eyes from his mother's side, quietly said, "Horses. Many horses. Steel shod. Coming in at a trot."

He hadn't finished before Longarm and Dutch spied the heads-down and dusty bays swinging through a gate held wide by a blurry rider on his own dusty cow pony. Two more blurry figures were riding drag to drive the small remuda the only way there was to go. As the thirteen bays in all trotted into the corral below and commenced to mill with nowhere else to trot, Dutch grinned like a mean little kid and raised his old Winchester Yellowboy to lever a round in the chamber as he decided, "We drop the two on the far side and shoot that pony out from under the one by the gate, that ought to give us one alive."

Longarm snapped, "Don't you dare! That's a direct order! Marshal Vail and the Powers-That-Be want their ringleaders, not an errand boy sent ahead on point so's some total asshole can give our position away!"

Dutch murmured, "Shit, can't you take a little joke? We're after that short stubby one with the Scotch plaid vest, right?"

Longarm said that was about the size of it as, sure enough, the rider by the gate swung it shut on the milling remuda and rode after his two companions, at a lope, until the three of them could get lost in the dusty sunglare and tricky shadows to the west. Smiley opined they'd cut around behind that big coal pile over in the Burlington yards.

Longarm said it didn't matter, repeating, "Hoss MacLeod surely sent small potatoes with no prior arrests for his opening gambit. You can hire many an out-of work herder, this side of Larimer Street, to drive most anything most anywhere, no questions asked, for pocket change. The sneaky Scotchman means to sit the first-dance out and see who else might have come to the ball."

So they waited, then waited some more, until Longarm was finding it tough to argue as Dutch kept saying things such as, "They're watching from some other vantage point, waiting for that sister of their pal to show her pretty face before they move any closer. They say Hoss MacLeod is a cautious thief and how smart would he have to be to notice there's nobody over this way but them lonesome ponies?"

Longarm stared soberly down at the dusty bare backs of the calmed-down riding stock as he decided, "You could be right. It happens. But whether a cautious horse thief suspects a trap or not, would he leave that much prime horseflesh to the gathering dusk or would he decide to take it back and see whether he could sell it somewheres else?"

Dutch started to say something stupid. But nobody working for Marshal Billy Vail was allowed to be totally stupid. So Dutch nodded and said, "Right. The least we can hope for is them same two-bit riders coming back for all that stock. MacLeod will expect us to arrest them before we allow them to just ride off with all that govenment property. Only, instead of arresting them here, we'll trail them and arrest *him*, there, wherever the sneaky son of a bitch is waiting for them!"

Longarm plucked a hay stemp to chew, dying for a smoke, as another million years went by and then four more riders were drifting in, walking their mounts in the hazy glare as, out in the yards, a switch engine commenced to rattle and bang freight cars all over creation.

Despit the tricky light, Smiley quietly observed, "Yellow and black plaid vest. The short one, second from our right on the buckskin."

Longarm told them to pretend they were stone gargoyles on some far away church as he resisted his own impulse to shift his own Winchester '73 into position. He knew that from the rider's vantage point the open hoist hatch of their hay loft was illuminated crisp and clear as crystal by the sunset's rays from *behind* them.

He murmured, "He's puzzled but not ready to give up such a sale. Let's hope he hopes Miss Alvina is watching from her own corner of the ballroom for someone else to begin the music."

The three lawmen waited, knowing other lawmen were watching from all around, as Hoss MacLeod and his three cronies rode to the gate but left it shut as they sat their own mounts on the far side, staring at the un- saddled stock in the corral between.

MacLeod took out a pocket watch, consulted it, and seemed to have bad things to say about making appoint- ments with womankind. Longarm knew the feeling. Few women read a compass or watch dial the way a man did. It wasn't that they didn't know how to tell time. Any man who showed up late with his flowers, book, or candy found out, soon enough, what a lady thought of any brute who'd turn up three minutes late. But just as many a married man felt that vow to forsake all others didn't apply to them, few women felt they had to be there on the hour, when an hour or so later would do just as well.

Longarm was hoping the four riders down below would move in closer. But then he saw Hoss MacLeod heave a resigned shrug and wheel his own mount the other way. As his followers moved to ride off with the son of a bitch, Longarm swung the muzzle of his saddle gun to train it their way as he called out, "That's far enough, MacLeod! Rein in and dismount and then grab for some sky if you ever hope to admire another sunset!"

The stubby MacLeod might have done as he was told. One of the men with him spun his pony like a top to slap leather and commence throwing pistol rounds, wild and wooly, until one of the other deputies posted on a warehouse roof to the south shot the silly bastard out of his saddle whilst all hell busted loose!

"Cease fire!" Longarm roared as another and then all four outlaw saddles were emptied by the fusilade from all sides. As the ragged gunfire subsided and the two deputies with Longarm could make out what he was saying, as if he meant it, Dutch protested, "I only fired twice and I never aimed at the one in the plaid vest, Pard!"

"Your mother still sucks off sheep herders for pennies and your daddy takes it in the ass for free!" Longarm snarled as he got up and then ran back to the loft ladder, tossing his Winchester down ahead of him as, behind him, Dutch pouted. "Aw, you didn't have to be so unkind! I swear I only fired at the one who was throwing lead at us!"

Longarm scooped up his Winchester from the wetter straw below and stomped outside and through the once more milling military stock as he assured nobody in particular that both their baby sisters had been knocked up by the hogs they rutted with in the sty out back.

He opened the far gate and shut it after him lest the stock mill on out as he moved on to inspect the damage in the dusty passage beyond.

The damage had been considerable. Their four ponies had run off, as one might expect any pony with a lick of sense to do at such time. But the four men who'd ridden in on them now sprawled like tossed out rag dolls, moaning and groaning some as the dust settled on them and their bleeding wounds.

The first one Longarm came to, the one who'd invited the gunplay with that ill-advised quick-draw, looked to be around nineteen and was surely dead as a turd in a milk bucket, having caught more rounds in a hurry than anyone else. Longarm moved on to the stubbier figure of Hoss MacLeod, facedown in the 'dobe dust and powdered horse shit, to roll the leader of the bunch on his broad back. MacLeod had lost his hat, to expose a bald pate, and his mustached face was flecked with blood where it wasn't caked with dust. His now dusty but still garish plaid vest had been punctured thrice, with one bullet hole bleeding bad. Longarm hunkered down with his Winchester across his things to feel the older man's throat. MacLeod opened his eyes and asked in a surprisingly conversational tone, "What happened? Who are you? Did you just shoot me?"

Longarm replied as laconically, "I was fixing to ask you what made you suspect something. I'd be the law, U.S. Deputy Marshal Custis Long. Might that vest be your family plaid, Mister MacLeod?"

The dying man replied with a slight burr, "MacLeod of Harris, and it's a *tartan*, damn it. A plaid is a sort of poncho one wears in the old country and I still want to know how come you just shot me."

Longarm calmly explained, "I never. You gents started it when that one old boy slapped leather. Unless you have wax in your ears, you must have heard me yelling at the four of you to surrender peaceable. It was my sincere intent to take you alive when I arrested you."

MacLeod blinked up at Longarm to decide, "I must have wax in my ears. It sounds as if you were talking about arresting me. On what charge, ye daft loon?"

Longarm said, "That's one of the reasons they wanted me to see if I could bring you in alive. The U.S. Cav and Colorado Guard are both mighty interested in those abused but well-bred bays on the far side of yonder corral gate, Mister MacLeod."

He saw Deputy Smiley opening said gate to join him as the dying man he'd hunkered over demanded in a tone of injured innocence, "What are you talking about? I don't know anything about those horses in yon corral. The four of us were just cutting through the stockyards on our way to Wazee Street when we saw the corral ahead of us blocked off and decided to ride around some other way. Then all of a sudden everybody was shooting at us and all of a sudden it's the gray piper I seem to be hearing somewhere down the glen."

Smiley rolled one of the others over. Longarm motioned him back and told MacLeod, "We've sent for a doc. You'll be all right. Just hang on and help me out with my officious report, like a sport. We both know you're facing some hard time for them hot horses you were trying to sell off this evening. But you can make it hard or easy time by helping us tidy up some loose ends."

MacLeod coughed blood, gasped for breath, and demanded, "What are you trying to pull, here? I never stole those horses. Kansas Red stole the damned horses, if you'd like to hurry up with that doctor and, now that I've had time to reconsider, that double-crossing little slut must have planned to ruin me from the beginning!"

"What is he talking about? He makes no sense?" said Deputy Smiley.

Longarm murmured, "Shut up! Let me see if I can sort something worthwhile out of his delirium. He just now mentioned the redhead they've had scouting for them!"

Hoss MacLeod stared bleary eyed and muttered, "Why has it gotten so dark so early? Why do you say Kansas Red was scouting for me? Didn't you just say I came here this evening to bid on these prime ponies? Kansas Red and *her* riders stole those military mounts from Camp Weld! Do I look dumb enough to raid military reservations, ye daft *Sássenach*?"

Longarm soberly replied, "Yep. Dealing in stolen horseflesh is still dealing in— Oh, shit, recieving stolen goods would be a lesser charge. So let's say that was a nice try. But I know for a fact you were never invited

53

here to bid on hot horseflesh by that notorious freckled-faced strawberry blonde. I stand ready to bear witness in open court that you came here this evening to meet up with a paid up member of the W.C.T.U. with taffy blonde hair and not a blemish to be seen on her vanilla ice-cream hide, anywheres above her garters. After that she stands as ready to swear *you* were the one who approached *her* with hot horseflesh for sale. So would you care to change your story before I have to turn it in on paper and stick you with it in court?"

MacLeod didn't answer. Longarm nudged him, felt the side of his throat and muttered, "Swell. The bastard's dead and if I ever find out who the stupid bastard was who put that fatal round in him I'll— Well I don't like to brag. So I'll save it for then."

Smiley shrugged and said, "He was a horse thief. He was a liar. When you call a man a horse thief you've already established that he's a liar. He was lying to the bitter end, trying to mix us up."

"He succeeded!" Longarm swore, closing the dead man's eyes and then getting to his feet as he added, "We've recovered the stolen stock. We seem to have killed at least one of the leaders. But why was he trying to get his scout, that strawberry blonde, in trouble just now?"

Smiley suggested, "He said she double-crossed him."

Longarm nodded, but asked, "How? Alvina Lockwood said another gal answering to the description we have on that mysterious redhead came to her hotel as if to make certain the deal was still on for this evening. Do you reckon that was what he was bitching about, just now?"

Smiley said, "I'd bitch if I sent a scout ahead and she led me into a trap, or I thought she had. That might be worth spreading. If the late Hoss MacLeod thought Kansas Red double-crossed the gang, who's to say what others might have to say about that, and what if she has enough common sense to come to us for safety?"

Chapter 7

It was well after moonrise before they had things halfway sorted out, and even then they had more questions than answers on their hands.

It was easy enough to dispatch Hoss MacLeod and his lesser lights to the County Morgue and, along the way, that trigger-happy follower of the reputed horse thief was identified as a hired gun wanted up Montana way for starting another shoot-out and winning. Colorado was pleased as punch that they had something on the late Hoss MacLeod aside from all those rumors and it would be easy enough to get a search warrant and go through his quarters and his own livery stable to the north to see what other mistakes he might have made.

Word was sent to the army remount service about the seven cavalry mounts they'd recovered. State troopers reclaimed the Colorado Guard stock on the spot.

But they didn't have Kansas Red, whatever her real name might be, and worse yet, MacLeod's dying remarks about the mysterious strawberry blonde didn't jibe with other witnesses, from the perimeter guards who said they'd spotted her scouting ahead of a raid to Alvina

Penn, who'd said Kansas Red had come to her hotel with a message from MacLeod.

Alvina's kid brother, Edward Lockwood, wasn't much help when Longarm traipsed to the County Jail to transfer him to the Federal House of Detention a couple of streets over. As the sleep-gummed young layabout got dressed he told Longarm he'd heard there was a bold gang of stock thieves with one or more gals on horseback scouting for them. But he'd heard anyone working for Hoss MacLeod make mention of them and volunteered that as the dying Scotchman had said, Hoss MacLeod had been a dealer in stolen goods who stayed close to home, rather than a far ranging outlaw who'd raided all up and down the Front Range in recent memory.

Once he had the self-confessed sneak thief dressed, Longarm broke out his handcuffs, saying, "Before you swear on your sister's honor or accuse me of cruel and unusual punishment, I've no more use for these orders than I have for this sissy tweed suit and tie they make me wear on duty here in town. But orders are orders if you expect to collect your pay and I have to make sure a desperado like you won't bust loose until he can be signed over to Federal Jurisdiction, officious."

So they left Lockwood's cell with the prisoner's right wrist cuffed to Longarm's left. That left Longarm's gun hand free and made it way easier to sign the infernal release forms out front in triplicate before they were out on the street in the crisp night air. Longarm said, "We're walking. This way. It ain't far enough for me to collect travel money on you and I'll be switched if you're worth cab fare from my own pocket. Gives us time to go over your fibs again in any case. Once I deliver you to Federal Jurisdiction they'll start putting everything you say down on paper and *then* how will you ever backtrack about Kansas Red?"

Lockwood protested, "I tell you I don't know anything about the gal. I was never a paid up member of MacLeod's bunch or any other. I was only born too sensitive to herd cows and too poor to support my chosen way of life without a little something extra now and again."

"Your sister says she tried to put you through college," Longarm replied as they headed on down the sandstone sidewalk, deserted like the most of the business district at that hour, save for an island of bright lights every quarter mile or so, where a saloon, a tobacco shop, or chili parlor still found it profitsome to stay open after quitting time.

Lockwood sighed and said, "I wouldn't be in this fix if Alvina hadn't cut back my allowance when I dropped out of school. She seems to think I'd just use anything she gave me on having a good time and I told you she's in the W.C.T.U. Those dried up old bags can't abide anybody else having any fun."

Longarm assumed Lockwood hadn't seen his elder sister naked, recent, and Alvina had explained she'd joined up for the tea parties. He told her sniveling kid brother, "Your motives for stealing that palomino are moot. Before you try to feed me any more bullshit, I want you to listen tight. I told your big sister I might be able to save you from hanging under Colorado Law and I just did, unless you piss Judge Dickerson off enough to have him transfer you back to Colorado as a useless federal witness. So when they take you before him, come morning, try not to be so useless. You may find this hard to accept, but hardly anybody but your poor sister gives toad squat about you, personal. We just want some more serious crooks, and arresting Kansas Red would be worth more than hanging you. So you'd better get to work on that memory you seem to be having so much trouble with, and you'd better have a better story for the judge when you appear before him. I don't make false promises. So I'll tell you true there's only a chance the judge will let you fly free as a bird in exchange for some serious fingering of more serious crooks. But it's a good chance. Say fifty-fifty. So you just study on that once we have you bedded down some more."

Lockwood muttered something about honor among thieves that inspired Longarm to snort, "You really must be new at the game. Men with honor don't steal things. To call a man an honest crook would be to describe a trail-town whore as a virgin. Hoss MacLeod just tried to sell Kansas Red to us as he lay dying. You're facing hard time with nothing to drink but water, if you're lucky, or a sudden snap at the end of a rope if you ain't, unless you sell her to us. So why are you acting so shy? You were never high enough in the organization to be getting any of that strawberry blonde, yourself."

Lockwood didn't answer or, if he did, Longarm never heard him, for just then a distant rifle squibbed and Longarm was crabbing sideways into a service entrance with Lockwood half off his feet in tow as, sure enough, that rifle ball, moving just a tad slower than the sound of it's black powder's big push, thunked wetly into human flesh.

Longarm couldn't tell where Lockwood had been hit. But from the way he went limp as a spent condom he'd been hit bad. So Longarm dragged the important parts of Lockwood into the meager cover of the locked up service entrance and uncuffed himself from his shot-up prisoner to risk a peek around the brick jamb as he got his own gun out.

Somewhere a police whistle was trilling and a faint whisp of gunsmoke was drifting into the glow of a street lamp from the flat rooftop of an otherwise dark and brooding office building, catty-corner across the way. Longarm braced his 44-40 in both hands with one wrist against the bricks, but held his fire as he waited to see whether the rooftop son of a bitch was willing to risk another shot from up yonder or mayhaps anywhere else.

Nothing happened until he'd been joined by two copper badges in blue. By good fortune one of them knew Longarm on sight and so they were saved a heap of tedious explanations and Longarm was free to bend over and make certain Lockewood was as dead as he was acting.

Once he had, he told the copper badges, "I was transfering this prisoner over to our house of detention. Somebody must not have wanted me to. It's up for grabs whether they were aiming at him or me."

One of the local lawmen opined, "It was most likely you. Had they nailed you, instead, along this deserted stretch, they'd have been able to rescue their pal, right?"

The other copper badge objected, "Wrong. They were after the one they were aiming for. This stretch ain't that deserted. *We* heard that shot and came running, didn't we? They were talking about Longarm and this case, earlier, at the precinct house."

He turned to ask Longarm if the dead man at their feet hadn't been a material witness, being transfered to federal custody.

When Longarm agreed that had been about the size of it, the copper badge smiled smugly and said, "There you go. Better to be sure than sorry. Shooting a man from a distance to shut him up would be way safer than shooting a lawman still cuffed to him, not knowing for certain if someone else was packing the key and how much time they had to work with, even then!"

The first one nodded thoughtfully and decided, "They'd know what a fix a live pal cuffed to a freshly shot lawman might find himself in, too. They'd know he'd be even more likely to talk with us beating the shit out of him so, yep, I reckon he made their most sensible target."

Longarm was too polite to say he wished all the answers were always so easy. He had it down as one of those puzzles where you needed some more pieces to make an educated guess.

Meanwhile they had another body for the meat wagon. Anyone shot dead on the streets of Denver went to the same county morgue long enough to be tagged and put on ice. County, State, or Federal authorities worked things out from there, lest things get stinky whilst they were making up their minds.

By that time it was late to come calling at anyone at home. But Longarm went back up Capitol Hill to knock on Billy Vail's front door in any case. The older lawman grumped to the door wearing his bathrobe and a darked scowl than usual as he greeted his late caller with, "This better be good, you infernal night owl!"

Longarm replied there were too many loose ends for them to wait until morning. So Vail led him back to the kitchen and sat him at a deal table while he commenced to build them a pot of coffee from scratch, saying, "My old woman is in a state of *dishabille*. That's fancy French for in bed with no clothes on and right now she's sore as hell at you. You sent word earlier about recovering them military mounts and gunning them three horse thieves. What's happened since?"

Longarm told him as Vail measured out a generous ration of Arbuckle brand hardwater-grind coffee. Longarm knew his wife didn't approve of his tobacco brand, either, but old Billy Vail was better at bossing others than being bossed. So that was likely the reason his old woman still slept buck-naked upstairs. It was a caution how married women tended to take up with delivery boys as soon as they had a husband housebroken to their expressed desires.

61

By the time Vail had heard Longarm out, he'd poked the coals in the kitchen range awake and had the pot of fresh brew perking. So he turned to light a stogie and have a seat at the table, himself, as he thoughtfully asked, "Just what do you reckon they were afraid that weak link, Lockwood, was about to tell us?"

Longarm shrugged and replied, "If I had the least notion they'd have had no call to shoot him. We can't even be certain they weren't aiming at me. Lockwood *said* he didn't know Kansas Red or any of those other far-ranging raiders. That don't prove shit. MacLeod was trying to tell other fibs about Kansas Red as he lay dying. He said he'd never stolen that remuda and was only there to bid on stock stolen by yet another gang Kansas Red-has been riding with."

Vail got his pungent black stogie going before he shook out the match and said, "He must not have known Alvina Penn nee Lockwood had already come forward with his offer to sell the hot horseflesh to her and *her* gang, meaning, what, that Edward Lockwood rode with other crooks?"

Longarm nodded and agreed, "That's how it reads to me, in large type. I'm still working on the footnotes. If there was any sincerity at all to MacLeod's suspicion he'd been set-up by Kansas Red, it might just be safe to assume MacLeod, Lockwood, that mysterious strawberry blonde and Lord knows who-all have been wheeling and dealing in hot horseflesh, in cahoots or in friendly rivalry. If MacLeod thought he was offering that last batch of mounts from Camp Weld to Lockwood's outfit, and that Kansas Red had pulled something sneaky, it commences to look more and more as if Edward Lockwood was fibbing about not knowing that strawberry blonde, and we do know she scouts ahead for serious outlaws."

Vail said, "I follow your drift. Let's drift her a tad

further. Let's see what we have if *everybody*'s been fibbing! Wouldn't it be dumb and reckless for anybody to run a whole remuda off their Camp Weld pasture and then offer them for sale to a sister they'd never met of a petty thief they'd dealt with on occasion?"

Longarm nodded soberly and replied, "To hear her tell, Hoss MacLeod didn't know her married name and hadn't heard she owned and operated a good-sized stock operation down to South Park, either. Her brother went along with her tale that they were no longer close enough for her to approve of his stealing horses. But we only have their words for that and one of them is dead."

"Now we're getting someplace," Vail chortled as he rose to check the coffee and decided it had perked enough to pour.

But as he fetched two mugs back to the table Longarm quietly asked, "Where have we got to, for certain? No matter how I reshuffle this deck I don't care for any of the hands I've dealt, so far. If we leap to the easy conclusion that brother and sister were really in cahoots, with him and his pals stealing stock and her disposing of it under her own registered brand after letting it cool off on her big old S Bar P, we have to figure out why she came forward to tell us where we'd be able to catch Hoss MacLeod red-handed. Did you forget her brother, Lockwood, was an associate of Hoss MacLeod?"

Vail sipped some coffee, strong and black as Longarm and other former range riders like it, before he pointed out, "I don't recall you telling me, earlier, that the dying MacLeod made any mention of Lockwood at all."

Longarm said, "Lockwood told me he'd sold stolen stock to MacLeod and Lockwood's sister, Miss Alvina, said MacLeod and a gal who surely describes as Kansas Red offered to sell *her* that hot horseflesh from Camp Weld."

Vail grimaced and said, "Them figures don't add up.

63

There's no way we can keep that shooting at the Kiowa Livery out of the morning papers but we might be able to sit on the story of her brother's death long enough for you to go down to Manitou Springs with our personal condolences as you watch the expression on her face."

Longarm frowned as he stirred nothing but air into his hot coffee to cool it, soberly asking, "What do we suspect her of?"

Vail shrugged and said, "That's for you to find out. When you can't get three different stories to jibe, somebody has to be lying, and that stock-dealing widow with a known horse thief in her family is the only storyteller still alive!"

Longarm tasted his coffee. It was hot enough and black enough but a tad weaker than he'd have brewed it. Old Billy had been trailing owlhoot riders from behind a desk a spell.

Vail asked, "What are you waiting for, a kiss goodbye? You have some trains to catch before dawn, old son."

Longarm said, "I'm way ahead of you on railroad time tables."

So Vail asked what he was grinning about and Longarm only replied, "I didn't know I was grinning, Boss."

He felt no call to tell an older married man what Alvina Penn nee Lockwood looked like in just those black lisle stockings.

Chapter 8

The D&RG dispatcher warned Longarm that their slow freights moving out after midnight ran slow indeed. But he didn't have too far to go.

He dropped off the caboose with his saddle and possibles at Colorado Springs, around eighty miles south, at sunrise, and had time to breakfast with fried eggs over chili con carne before he caught the narrow-guage west for the short hop to Manitou Springs, just northeast of Pikes Peak.

Had real Indians named the springs along the Fountain Creek canyon, they'd have likely used the local Ute term for Medicine, pronounced something like "Poo Ha." "Manitou" was one of those Hiawatha-Minni-Ha-Ha "Indian" names white real estate speculators came up with. "Ma-tou" wasn't too far off the term Arapaho, Cheyenne, and other Algonquin dialects used for a notion white poets and hopeful missionaries got all wrong. No stone-age folk, Red, Yellow, Black, or White had ever come up with anything as organized as even the pagan religions of the old world. Folk had to know how to read and write before they could agree halfway on holy scriptures with "Great Spirits" and such. So Puha,

Ma'tou, Wakan Tonka, and such translated more honestly as "Great Mysterious Medicine," which was close as your average medicine man, way chanter, dream singer, or whatever you wanted to call him, or her, could get.

So Manitou Springs had been named by Doctor William Bell, who still bottled and sold the natural soda water he'd admired there just a few years back. Then the narrow-guage, running on over the Front Range for the South Park decided that made a swell get-off-and-gape stop for their Pikes Peak tourist trade, situated as it was betwixt the northeastern slopes of Pikes Peak and a bodacious rock pile they'd decided to call "The Garden Of The Gods."

Longarm agreed that was an improvement over a failed attempt to turn the Garden Of The Gods into one hell of a big beer garden. Leaving the slopes of Pikes Peak and the imposing stone fantasy of the Garden Of The Gods more natural, local establishments catering to the tourist trade and surrounding country folk had mushroomed out from the core of a young but growing Manitou Springs from the intersection of east-west Manitou Avenue and north-south Canyon Avenue, with Doc Bell's red sandstone castle on Manitou and the almost as imposing town house of Alvina Lockwood over on Grand Avenue, running into Canyon just north of the post office.

Longarm left his McClellan saddle, Winchester, and saddlebags packed with possibles in care of Western Union, once he'd sent a wire up to his Denver office, knowing old Billy would be at his desk by now. Then he ambled on up to the Penn mansion, slow, aware that not everyone on Earth shared Billy Vail's views on rising with the roosters and beating the sunrise to work.

As he checked the house numbers and saw where they were leading him in the now-bright morning sunlight,

Longarm had second thoughts about the traveling duds he'd changed into before hopping that slow freight in Denver.

Since President Rutherford B. Hayes and his even fussier First Lady, Miss Lemonad Lucy, had been setting the standards for proper attire in and about federal offices, Longarm had been forced to report for work at the Denver Federal Building dressed like an infernal ribbon clerk, or at least a prosperous cattleman, in a suit and vest, with a shoestring necktie, over his stovepipe boots and cross-draw gun-rig. But, out in the field, for the same reasons he toted that old army saddle along, Longarm often got away with the clean but faded blue denim jeans and jackets he had on that morning, over a sailcloth workshirt the color of well-broken-in throw-rope. So he had to wonder, as he crossed over to the mansart roofed fresh-painted frame with an octagonal corner tower, whether Miss Alvina would feel he was shaming her by pounding on her front door instead of going around to the back. When the lady of any house kept her siding painted canary yellow, with her trim a stark white that had to be repainted every other year at the least, she was a house-proud lady concerned with appearances indeed. And, in that hotel room up Denver way, she'd doubtless felt under less pressure from her neighbors as she fought to save her brother.

But it was too late and too public to change clothes, now. So he went on through her well-kept front yard and up the steps to twist the brass knob of her doorbell.

An old geezer in butler's livery came to the door to look dismayed as Longarm flashed his badge and ID, asking if he could speak to the lady of the house. The old butler shook his head, but before Longarm could get sore, he explained how Miss Alvina was over at the S Bar P in the South Park country, supervising a search for strays. The butler said he had no notion when his boss lady might be back. Longarm felt certain that was true when the butler added that Miss Alvina had been off hunting strays in the high country for nigh on a week, now.

Longarm didn't ask if the gal he'd seen off on that earlier train with a French kiss had dropped by her town house in Manitou Springs on her way further west. Old Alvina could tell him when he caught up with her why she didn't want her own house servants to know where she was, or, leastwise, not to tell anybody where she might be, if they knew.

He thought about that from both sides after he'd thanked the older man and headed back to the nearby center of town. Billy Vail wanted him to talk nice to that dead horse thief's only known living kin, not to crawfish her further from the possible truth by scaring her with a search warrant.

If she was hiding out in that big town house, possibly watching from that imposing tower with a spy glass, she'd know by now he was in town and, what the hell, back in Denver she'd allowed she was willing to meet him more than halfway. So his first move would be to give her a while to get in touch with him. Hanging around town a spell instead of tear-assing over to the South Park might give him the opportunity to gossip with her neighbors about her. Manitou Springs wasn't big enough to keep many secrets from determined small town gossips and it would be smart to find out whether Alvina had a rep for straight talk or drawing the long bow before he talked to her some more about the Late Hoss MacLeod and the mysterious Kansas Red.

Dropping by the Western Union again, Longarm sent another progress report and offered the one clerk on duty a couple more three-for-a-nickel cheroots. The tow-haired kid had said he'd keep that saddle and such under the counter for free. But Longarm didn't like to let folk feel he was taking advantage of them.

While he was there, he resisted the impulse to ask the town's only telegrapher what they thought of a likely important steady customer. Whether Alvina Penn nee Lockwood was honest as the day was long or slippery as an eel in a spitoon, nobody who wired back and forth to the outside world about beef prices and stock futures would cheat any nationwide Western Union, when they only charged a nickel a word.

He refrained from calling on the town law for better reasons than that. He knew that once he made a courtesy call on the town law all the gossips in town would know a federal lawman had come down from the capitol to poke about the Penn and Lockwood dirty linen. Longarm had learned the hard way in other small towns how many spiteful fibs you heard about ladies, pure as the driven snow, from the enemies nobody in a small town could avoid making. It didn't matter whether you were a Republican or Democrat, wet or dry, church-going or free thinking. As long as you had any opinions of your own, somebody was agin 'em.

The Western Union office was open for business around the clock. The small store-front saloon across the way stayed open around the clock because gents prosperous enough to send business wires needed handy places to wait for replies. But there were no other customers at the bar when Longarm strode in. It was just as well. For the lone barkeep laughed at him when he ordered a sarsaparilla soda.

When the small town barkeep asked if his establishment looked like a damned drugstore, Longarm explained, "It ain't for my usual self. I have to scout up the boss lady of your local W.C.T.U. in the name of the law and I don't want tobacco or strong spirits on my breath."

The barkeep suggested he sip some crème de menthe instead. He said, "We don't serve sarsaparilla or any other soft drinks. But the smell of the alcohol gets lost amid all that mint liqueur."

So Longarm ordered a shot of the sickly sweet green goo and, as he'd hoped, the barkeep naturally knew who was running the local chapter of an outfit dedicated to running him out of business.

The Steamboat Gothic town house of Mrs. Prunela Bleeker on Ruxton Avenue sort of looked down its front steps on the rest of things from the giddy heights of Ruxton Heights. The widow Bleeker, described to him as a saloon-closing shrew who just needed a good stiff screwing to calm her down, had chosen a practical park-bench green for the trim of her mustard mansart-roofed mansion, but felt the need of a tower at all four corners to indicate her social position in that particular frog pond.

Her butler was younger, snootier, and told Longarm to go around to the service entrance if he was there to fix that cellar door.

Longarm fished his badge and ID a second time as he mildly told the simpering servant, "We can do this friendly or I can come back with the town law and you have my word I'll see they hold you a good seventy-two hours on suspicion of mopery."

That worked. It usually did. Not a feather merchant in a hundred knew that "mopery" was lawman's jargon meant to cover pains in the ass who hadn't done anything in particular but ought to be tossed in the tank for a spell to teach them some damned respect.

Not wanting to be charged with the same, and afraid to ask what it might be, the snooty butler allowed he'd see if Madame was receiving.

A few minutes later it turned out she was, and Longarm was surprised to find Prunela Bleeker, despite her position, looking down upon most of Manitou Springs, was another handsome young widow woman, with black hair, sloe eyes, and features that would have seemed more natural on a French maid than the lady of the house.

He was sorry he was wearing faded denim but glad he'd swished his mouth out with crème de menthe as she stuck out the back of a paw for him to kiss, it seemed, since she didn't seem to mind as she took her paw back and waved him to a maroon plush sofa in her front parlor.

She was wearing a low-cut velveteen outfit of the same color. You could tell a gal had money when her duds, upholstery, and wallpaper flowers were the same shade of maroon.

When he set his Stetson aside and tried to show her his credentials, the sultry local leader of the W.C.T.U. trilled, "Jason has already told me the famous Custis Long has called on us in the name of the law! I can't wait to tell the others about this exiting visit from a famous lawman! You *are* the Custis Long they call Longarm, the one who shot it out with that state senator in the capitol dome that time?"

To which Longarm modestly replied, "Just doing my job, ma'am, and I'd be much obliged if we could keep this visit to ourselves for just a spell."

She yanked a bellpull and sat down beside him on the same sofa as she gasped, "You mean you're on a secret mission, and you've called on *me* for help?"

Longarm nodded soberly and, praise the Lord, a maid coming in to ask what Madame wanted gave him time to choose his words carefully. A lawman questioning a witness had to sort of play the unknown quality on the line, like an undetermined fish in murky water, lest he spook the truth off the hook with an ill-chosen question.

So once his brunette hostess told the maid to rustle

71

them up some refreshments and they were alone some more, Longarm told her in a sly and confidential tone, "I'm trying to cut the trail of a confidence man. A Bible-thumping crook who takes advantage of decent Christian women by pretending to be a preaching man, dedicated to the temperance cause. We've reason to suspect he's been working his wicked game out our way. He made a big mistake in the Indian Territory a spell back, though. He cheated some Baptist ladies of the Cherokee Persuasion, and that made it a federal offense, see?"

She stared at him like a thrilled owl to whisper back, "Oh, this is so exiting! What did this monster *do*? How did he take advantage of those poor Christian squaws?"

So Longarm fed her a fable he made up as he went along about a two-faced preacher man worming his way into the good graces of unsuspecting church ladies with his handsome profile, oily charm, and ability to quote scripture, like the Devil, for his own purposes. He commenced to lay it on thicker as he saw she was not only buying it but enjoying a good excuse to hear dirty stories. Longarm fell back on dirty stories he'd heard from other church ladies about handsome devils who seduced choir girls, or boys, ran off with minister's wives, mother superiors, or most any poor innocent unprepared by her praying for such predators. He had to give his fictitious villain a name. So he warned her to look out for the Reverend Percival Wallburton and, when she laughed and said that sounded like a made-up name, he nodded gravely and told her, "He's worked his same wicked games amongst Papists as a Father Kenmore and told Mormon ladies he's the Danite Jonah on a secret mission from the Salt Lake Temple. So far, we've never heard of him pretending to be a Rabbi, but we fear it's only a question of time, if we don't put a stop to the fiend's wicked ways!"

That maid came back with a silver salver piled with

a tea service and enough cold cuts to open a small delicatessen. Prunela ordered her to set it down in the tower study they could see through a sliding door in one corner of the tower as she took Longarm by one hand and rose to suggest they carry on the rest of their private conversation behind a barred door.

The octagonal tower room's sunny windows all around were veiled with Irish lace curtains and maroon velvet drapes. As she locked the sliding doors after her maid, Longarm casually allowed he could use a list of all the members of her W.C.T.U. chapter who might be widow women, living alone, like her ownself. It seemed a sure bet he'd be able to narrow the gossip down to Alvina Penn nee Lockwood without letting on he was interested in her in particular.

The widow woman he found himself alone with in a sunny little room nobody could see in or out of sat him down on a leather chesterfield by the rosewood coffee table the salver was set on as she confided, "I can only think of two other members in my lonely state, thank heavens. Are you suggesting this dreadful preacher man preys on defenseless widows living alone?"

When Longarm suggested that was about the size of it, Prunela Bleeker didn't pour them any tea. She placed a hand on his thigh, closer to his crotch than his knee, to ask him in a low-down dirty voice to tell her what that other rascal did to lonely gals he managed to find his wicked self alone with.

Chapter 9

Having toted a badge for a spell, Longarm wasn't as surprised to have a church lady feeling him up some. As a lawman, he'd been called in often enough to suspect there was something about dwelling on sin more than most that got on church ladies' nerves. For it sure beat all how much slap and tickle could take place in a choir loft or rectory cellar after hours.

But Billy Vail had sent him down yonder to question Alvina Penn nee Lockwood, not to play slap and tickle with another widow woman entire. So he pretended not to notice her teasing hand as he asked about those other defenseless members of her flock.

She moved her hand a sneaky inch as she confided that only one of the other young widows was in town at the moment. She said, "I heard that awful Alvina Penn is over at her cattle spread in the South Park, bossing her poor cowboys around."

"How come you say this Alvina gal is awful, ma'am?" he asked, grabbing casually for the brass ring she'd just swung them around to.

The sultry Prunela moved her hand another inch as she calmly told him, "She's a holier-than-thou hypocrite.

Thinks the rest of us don't know she married that awful Sid Penn for his money! The rude, crude cow thief smelled like a goat and swore like a teamster at social gatherings. He drank like a fish alone, as well, to hear the trashmen who collected all those bottle deposits tell. Yet, to hear Alvina, these days, her dirty old man was some sort of plaster saint who'd somehow managed to leave her pure as well as sober! I mean, honestly, Custis, how many men do you know who respect their wives too much to want to fuck them?"

Longarm sobely replied, "I don't know any married-up men I'd have any call to ask, Miss Prunela. Did you just call this unusual husband a cow thief, as well?"

She replied without hesitation, "*My* late husband did, a lot, but he could never prove Sid Penn had helped himself to any Lazy L calves in those early roundups he liked to start without the rest of us. Some say he got water rights in the South Park with false promises to the Indians when it was still Ute country, too. Promised them he'd keep other whites out if they let him file a homespread claim on Indian land."

Longarm wanted to hear more about that other widow woman's stock spread in the high country, but he noticed the one he was alone with at the moment seemed to be messing with his fly buttons, now.

So, not wanting her to think he was too shy to mention it, he put a gentle hand on her wrist to calmly say, "You'd better let me unbutton my jeans if you're really all that interested, ma'am. Opening copper buttons on tight Levis can be tough on a lady's nails."

She blushed becomingly and replied, "Oh, dear me, I didn't notice I was fiddling so forward! I fear you distracted me with all that talk about Alvina Penn. Do you think it's really possible for a man and woman to sleep together in the same bed without . . . touching one another?"

He left her hand between his thighs as he unbuttoned his fly for them as he calmly replied, "Not hardly. Not conscious, leastways. I find it hard to keep my mind and mortal flesh off the topic when I'm alone on a chester-field with a pretty lady!"

She purred, "So I've heard!" as she took the matter in hand to stroke it even harder, asking, "Is it true you once had this naughty thing in Sarah Bernhardt, you romantic rascal?"

Longarm was less confused about her forward nature now. That cuss who'd first said it paid to advertise had been on the money and some gals sure liked to brag on screwing somebody other gals had heard of.

Thanks to those fool newspaper reporters who'd run out of lies to tell about James Butler Hickok since Cock-eyed Jack McCall had put a sudden end of those legendary exploits, they'd promoted him to top gunslick of the high plains and Calamity Jane hadn't been the first or last wild woman to make up brags about bedding the wildest man in the west.

But he owed it to the Divine Sarah to confess, "I was only assigned to body-guard her during an American tour of her traveling show, Miss Prunela."

The American gal who'd asked about a national trea-sure of France was unable to answer with her mouth full, kneeling mighty friendly between Longarm's knees as she blew an enthusiastic hunter's call on the French horn.

But before he could come in her mouth she'd slid up the front of him in her velveteen dress to hoist her ma-roon skirts and straddle the saliva-slicked shaft she'd sucked to full attention and impale herself on the same, having nothing on under the summerweight outfit.

"Oh, what are you doing to me, you brute?" She moaned as she leaned against him to add in a softer tone,

"Get those fucking buttons down the back of this bodice, damn it!"

So he did as she moved her wide-spread crotch up and down until he had them both half undressed by the time he came in her.

She gasped, "Ooh, I felt that and I want you to do it again!"

So he did, after taking it out long enough to undress her total and mount her face-to-face on the smooth, tufted leather, with her on the bottom with her high button shoes hooked over his bare shoulders to either side while she bumped and ground and assured him she never did this with just anybody, but seeing he was the law and they were on a secret mission together . . .

He learned another of her secrets when they paused for breath to sprawl naked on the chesterfield and she served them some refreshments. The cold cuts and soda crackers tasted like most free lunches one could expect in a first-class saloon. Her tea tasted way stronger than Billy Vail's coffee until you figured out where it got its kick. She demurely described it as "Irish Tea," albeit the bourbon it was laced with wasn't Irish whiskey. He didn't ask how that jibed with her being the head of the local W.C.T.U. Her fellow member, Alvina, had already explained how a small town widow might join up for the tea and gossip. He wondered idly what this widow would say if he told her that other widow had asked him right out to fuck her. He knew Prunela would tell all the other gals in her chapter about his visit, whether this was supposed to be a secret mission or not. Any man who talked about any lady behind her back was not only a cad but a total asshole. It always got back to a gal when you said anything good or bad about her.

As he washed down some ham and cheese on crackers with laced tea, Longarm asked about that other young widow Prunela had mentioned. The one there in town.

She grabbed for his limp love muscle in a possessive manner as she asked if he didn't know all the girls he needed to know in Manitou Springs.

He answered, easily, "Not hardly. I ain't up to knowing the rest of your chapter quite *this* well, Miss Prunela. But I told you why I had to make notes on all the likely victims of that crooked preacher man."

So she gave him a name he didn't bother to write down or commit to serious memory, seeing he was only trying to distract her from any suspicion he might be more interested in Alvina Penn nee Lockwood.

Being interested in that sweet, warm taffy blonde would have been easy, even if Billy Vail hadn't sent him down this way to interview her some more about hot horseflesh. For having enjoyed the sultry Prunela to the hilt, he found himself wondering what it would have been like if he'd taken that other young widow up on her offer at the Tremont House.

Prunela Bleeker was about as pretty, in a different way, with a more olive complexion, a thicker mop of brunette lap fuzz, and a somewhat different way of curving in and out. He couldn't be sure, having never run more than admiring eyes over the vanilla hide of Alvina, which of them had the softer skin or tighter twat. But the thinking along those lines got a man to twitching some, and so Prunela, feeling what she had a gentle grip on, commenced to stroke it gently as she sipped some tea and bourbon with her free hand, calmly marveling, "So it's true what they say about Longarm and I'm so glad! I was afraid those girls who'd boasted about bedding you were making up fairy tales that came true. One so often meets a Prince Charming who turns out to be just another fucking frog. The part I liked best about the tales they tell about you, Custis, is that we have to take their word for what you did to them with this marvel of nature because you never kiss and tell!"

Longarm washed down the last of his nibble with the last of his cupful as he promised not to tell if they went at it dog-style, now.

She protested, "In broad daylight, with you able to see my . . . you know what?"

"Asshole is the word you're groping for." He replied agreeably as he took her in his arms again to run his free hand down between her naked thighs and beyond, observing, "I'd be surprised as hell if you didn't have an asshole, Miss Prunela. I got one, too, as has Queen Victoria if she ever uses her chamber pot at all. I've never understood why we're supposed to say limb instead of leg or breast instead of tit. Does calling something by another name change what it looks like? Do you reckon that if I dog-styled you in the dark I'd picture you as a natural freak who never has to take a shit?"

She told him he was just horrid. Then she laughed dirty and rolled off the chesterfield to assume the position on the rug, with her elbows locked, her spine swayed, and her shapely rump thrust up at the dappled sunlight through the curtains to spangle her bare flesh with dancing stars as she smiled archly over a bare shoulder to ask him how he liked her twitching anal opening, and how it compared with that of Miss Sarah Bernhardt.

Longarm didn't deny any certain knowledge of any other lady's asshole as he knelt on the thick Persian rug to grab a hip bone in either hand and haul the curious widow on like a glove.

She hissed in pleasure, then suggested, "Silly, you have it up my pussy again!"

Longarm just kept thrusting as he replied, "That was where I was aiming it, ma'am. Despite what you might have heard about more exotic surroundings, it can get sort of disgusting if you do it without at least a sink with running water handy."

She lowered her cheek to the rug, purring, "I might have expected you to know about such matters. Have you ever seen that book from India they call the Kama Sutra, you naughty boy?"

He commenced to hump faster as he confided, "You can pick up a copy in most any penny arcade since it's been reprinted in this country, Miss Prunela. But as a once-married woman you surely know a lot of them fool positions just won't work, when real people try to get into them."

She laughed in a more open, healthy way and said, "It's such a relief to hear such a notorious fuck-master say that! I was so worried there might be something wrong with me. I know you're going to find this hard to accept, but a healthy young woman has needs and you're not exactly the only other man I've . . . experimented with since my poor Leonard was taken from me by that plague of spotted fever we had, summer before last."

Longarm agreed she seemed like a natural woman. She began to thrust her rump in time with him as she confided, "It takes a natural man, a lot of natural man, to satisfy my natural needs. I've hoped, in vain, to sort of . . . keep things going with some of those odd positions in that ancient Hindu tome. But when you get down to brass tacks, nothing beats keeping at it until you can come in a comfortable position, with a man who knows how to keep going. How do you keep going so long, dear?"

He shrugged his bare shoulders as he thrust his bare hips and told her, "I just like to screw women more than I like to drink or smoke and I just love to drink and smoke. I don't know as there is any secret, Miss Prunela. I do know that *worrying* about performing with say a new gal in town can make it tougher to get it up. I had the good fortune when I was very young, no more than twenty or so, to fail total in a hayloft, just as I had a gal I'd been after for days on her back in the dark with her legs spread wide and her old ring-dang-doo slick and wet in welcome."

"You call that *good fortune*?" the older woman he was enjoying in a happier here-and-now demanded, taking his full erection to the bottom of the well as she added, "Whatever did that poor girl say?"

Longarm replied with a sheepish chuckle, "She never spoke to me again, of course. Once I'd taken her back to the dance, cooled down, and back in control of such feelings, she left the dance early with another boy and Lord only knows whether he got any or not. For I was so ashamed I rode on without asking. I was on my way further west in any case. But as soon as I'd had time to study on what had happened, I felt a whole lot better and since that time I've seldom worried about whether I was going to be able to get it up or not."

She suggested that as long as he had it up she'd enjoy it more if they finished on the chesterfield, in a more intimate position. So they did and she didn't ask about that other time with another gal in another place until they'd savored another long shuddering orgasm.

Then, being a woman, she naturally wanted to know why he'd been so pleased about failing to get an erection just as he'd been about to put it in that sweet young thing in the hay loft.

Longarm fumbled a smoke from his shirt on the floor as he explained, "Had I been as old as thirty, in bed with somebody more serious, I'd have surely thought old age had snuck up on me to take the lead out of my pencil. I know that my first fear at the age of twenty was that I was past my prime as a natural man. So I was fixing to go see a sawbones about my poor pecker. Then I got to considering the questions he was likely to ask me. I knew he'd ask how long I'd been in that cow town after getting paid off at the end of a drive and he'd naturally want to know how much hell I'd been raisin' on how much sleep, and so forth and then it came to me I didn't need no sawbones. I needed a few hours of sleep, at least one warm meal, and enough time for my poor pecker to recover from the cow-town gals I'd had it in *before* I ever carried that waitress I'd been admiring in the meantime to that dance."

The mature woman he'd just satisfied laughed incredulously and asked, "You'd been paid off in a cow town at the end of a long dusty drive and no idea why you couldn't get it up?"

He lit the cheroot and shook out the match as he replied, "I told you I was young and foolish. But facing the fact that there are simply times you just don't feel up to it can keep a man from acting old and foolish."

So after they'd rested some he did it to her one more time before he explained he had to question other widow women and excused himself to go hire a horse. It was still early in the day and thanks to that last effort in that brunette widow, he doubted that sweet, soft taffy blonde widow Billy Vail had sent him after would be able to take any unfair advantage of him.

Chapter 10

When Longarm got back down to the Western Union, walking sort of stiff, he was told another stranger in town had been there asking for him. When Longarm asked what the other man had looked like the telegraph clerk said, "Morose. Dressed like an undertaker, save for his black Stetson, Justin boots, and the cross-draw six-gun under his coat."

Longarm said, "Sounds like one of the lawmen I ride with, up Denver way. Was he with a shorter, more cheerful-looking cuss?"

The Western Union man said, "He was with somebody. His sidekick stayed out front, holding their horses. I told the one who came in that you'd said you'd be back."

Longarm asked for his saddle. As the clerk hefted it over the counter to him, Longarm said, "Had to be Smiley and Dutch. But I wonder why my boss sent them down in person without wiring me whatever it was they're supposed to tell me."

He swung the heavily laden McClellan off the counter, adding, "I've got to find me a livery nag to load all this shit aboard. If my pals come back before I can bump noses with 'em outside, would you tell 'em the widow woman our boss sent me to see ain't in town, and that I'm on my way out to her S Bar P in the South Park if they'd like to catch up with me?"

The Western Union clerk allowed he would. They shook on that and parted friendly. Longarm kept an eye out for Smiley and Dutch but failed to spot anyone he knew on the streets of Manitou Springs as he made his way to the nearest livery, where he hired two ponies, a paint and chestnut with white stockings for two bits a day, apiece, with the livery waiving the usual deposit, seeing he was a known quantity riding for Uncle Sam.

He mounted the paint to lead the chestnut the first hour of his ride toward Ute Pass on to the South Park country. He knew Ute Pass was an easy eight or a hard four hour's ride. He had no idea how deep into the South Park he'd be heading, since they were not talking about what city slickers thought of as a park when they used the term as it was usually meant in the Colorado high country.

Yellowstone and other national parks in the west were parks in the sense of the French word, "*Parc*," albeit way bigger than most such public pleasures. But when Colorado riders referred to Estes Park, North Park, South Park, and such they were talking about the lay of the land, high in the sky, but relatively flat and open, betwixt the jagged-ass ridges of the complexicated Rocky Mountains, more a considerable crumple-up of the continental crust than the tidy domino row of snow-capped peaks that one could get, back east, just looking at postcards. The Front Range, including Pikes Peak, was a bodacious mountain range in its own right. But still just a sort of tag-along rise following the trend of the Continental Divide the way a pilot fish, a big pilot fish, might swim alongside a whale-shark. So there were miles and miles of rolling open grasslands, greener, with more water than the shortgrass prairies east of the foothills of the Front Range. Longarm had been told in town to swing south on the near side of Lake George and follow the survey trail blazed back in the Grant administration by the Hayden expedition. They'd naturally found greener pasture beyond some ash flats and after the country had been properly mapped, a Widow Hornbeck and her kids had filed and improved the first homestead claim, just south of that dusty dry stretch. Sidney Penn and others since had forged on further into once wild Indian country to file their own claims. Longarm figured he was facing the coming night and a good part of the next day in the saddle, unless he got lucky and met that sweet, soft taffy blonde on her way back to town. He found it sort of puzzling that a gal waiting on a brother fixing to get out of jail would be off hunting strays right now. He suspected there had to be something more than that to the story. But, what the hell, Billy Vail had sent him down her way to poke his nose in the lady's beeswax and once he caught up with her, he'd just *ask* her why she'd been talking and behaving so odd.

Following the post road west out of Manitou Springs he passed the usual outlying shanty towns, pig and chicken farms, hard-scrabble truck gardens and such you usually saw within easy carting distance of a growing town out that way. After that the weeds grew rank and goat-grazed betwixt the stumps of all the firewood gathered within an easy haul to Manitou Springs and the bigger Colorado Springs, a tad further east of Pikes Peak. But by the time he'd switched his saddle and his weight to the chestnut for a spell, they were starting to ride through patches of shade where aspen, at least, had sprouted as second grown beside the trail.

He rode on with mixed feelings, not looking forward to telling a lady her kid brother had been murdered, but curious as all get-out about the mixed signals Alvina

Penn nee Lockwood seemed to send. He was starting to recover from his morning romp with Prunela Bleeker, but he didn't think it likely he'd have to rise to the occasion for at least another forty miles and she had asked right out, bless her vanilla ice-cream hide.

From time to time he met other travelers headed east along the trail. But nobody seemed out to overtake him as he rode on west. He paused on each rise he topped for a look-see back the way he'd come, but if old Smiley and Dutch were trying to catch up they sure rode slow for U.S. deputy marshals.

Later that afternoon he rode into the settlement of Woodland, where the narrow-guage line running more or less the same direction as the post-road came to its last stop. The grades further west rose a whole lot steeper and that was why there was just the post-road over Ute Pass.

Longarm stopped in Woodland to rest his hired ponies, wash down some ham, eggs, and service-berry pie with strong black coffee, and give old Smiley and Dutch more time to catch up, if they were trying to.

When they failed to show up after he'd dallied a full hour at the end of the narrow-guage line, Longarm rode on, muttering. For he aimed to be over the pass and down out of the night winds before he called it a day by the side of the trail.

Few peaks of the Front Range rose above Timber Line and Ute Pass was naturally lower. So he'd worked his way a tad high for aspen but had plenty of spruce for shade as he consulted his pocket watch to decide they weren't too far east of the pass, if only a body could see worth shit amid all these overgown Christmas trees. He reined in near a big granite outcrop and told his ponies, "You boys enjoy a breather whilst I have a look around from up yonder, hear?"

Neither livery mount answered as they lowered their

muzzles as one to crop trailside sedge and wild onion greens. But he tethered them to low spruce boughs lest they plot against him whilst his back was turned.

Having no call for it, as far as he suspected, Longarm left his Winchester in its saddle boot as he scrambled up the outcrop for a better view all around.

Once he had, it was a hell of an improvement. Through the treetops to the west he could make out the notch of Ute Pass, about where he'd hoped it might be. Back the other way, he had a better view of the trail he'd been following. So he could make out two other riders moving up the grade from the east, now.

He muttered, "Well, it's about time!" and drew his .44-40 to fire a signal, then wave his hat as the riders in the distance reined in to peer up the slope his way, into the low afternoon sun.

After he'd waved like hell and sent another cloud of gunsmoke high, he saw they'd figured out where he might be and started riding closer. He lost sight of them as they closed the gap because there were more tree branches in the way now. But he could see clearly down the trail a furlong or more, closer in, so he stayed put, waiting for them to appear some more and tell him what in thunder Billy Vail wanted.

Nothing happened for quite a spell, as Longarm stood there against the cloudless cobalt sky, staring down into the park-bench green tangle of spruce branches. Then Longarm spotted a flash of movement off the trail, to his north, and then he wasn't there anymore, just as the sneaky son of a bitch fired a rifle round through the space Longarm had been standing like a big-ass bird.

They'd invited a younger Custis Long to a war they were having before he could finish school. So the education he'd been given in classrooms called Shiloh, Cold Harbor, and such had taught him to move sudden and move unpredictable whenever things didn't look natural, and neither Smiley, Dutch, or any other friend trying to overtake him with a message would have any natural reason to dismount and pussyfoot through the woods at a pal like that.

Since most any injury had a bullet-wound beat, Longarm had chanced throwing himself to the winds off the upslope side of the outcrop and, as chance would have it, heaps of spruce needles and dead busted branch wood had piled up at the upslope base of the boulders to break his fall. Sort of. It still knocked the wind out of him and he was fighting like hell to get it back as he forged further upslope through the trees, reloading his six-gun and wishing it was his Winchester all the way to a fallen forest giant overgrown with moss.

He dove over in and rolled back, tossing his hat aside to risk a peek over the angle formed by a thick dead branch of the fallen spruce.

He barely had his breath back by the time a figure afoot in funereal black hollowed the muzzle of a scope-sighted Schneider around the north face of that granite outcrop, sweeping his eyes and rifle muzzle back and forth up the slope. He did indeed look to have some Mex or Indian blood, but he wasn't Deputy Smiley by half. So Longarm braced his gun hand on the mossy log and fired, aiming low to compensate for the way one tended to shoot over a downhill target.

His heavy-enough 44-40 round folded the stalking rifleman over his belt buckle and deposited him on his side in that brush pile, jack-knifed around a heap of pain, to hear him holler.

A distant voice called, "Did you get him, Chief?"

The breed yelled back, "I'm git! Kill him for me, old son!"

By that time, Longarm, up and running with his hat back on, reloaded his revolver as he beelined up the slope as fast as he could manage. He knew the one left would try to circle wide to move in on the upslope side of that outcrop. He had the advantage of knowing he didn't have to worry about someone else having beaten him higher through the deep forest shade. So he just kept moving until he was as far upslope as a pistol ball would carry and then, spotting a hammock of fern between two close-set tree trunks, he took cover some more.

He'd barely done so when he detected motion off to his south and just forgot about breathing till he had a bead on another black suit, worn by a younger cuss with a weak-chinned pure-white profile. The bastard was packing a Remington repeating .45-70 that could carry way further than Longarm's handgun. So Longarm emptied half his wheel into the son of a bitch before that could become a problem.

He was pleased as well as surprised by the results as he reloaded before he rose to move to where the rascal lay face down in an awkward sprawl. He'd hoped with any luck to hit his target at least once at close to fifty yards. He saw, as he rolled the limp cuss over, he'd put one through the rib cage from side to side, one through the guts, high up, and pinked the far thigh to leave him with a temporary limp, had he lived.

"Did you get him?" a distant voice called. So Longarm picked up the fallen foreman's rifle to mosey on down the slope being its muzzle, aiming from the hip as he held the Remington in his one hand with the double-action sixgun in the other.

As the first one came back into view, Longarm saw the cuss had both knees up against his chest with his eyes squeezed tight and blood oozing from one corner of his mouth. The breed seemed about done for. But he could hear Longarm's boot heels crunching spruce needles well enough to groan, "Jesus H. Christ I'm hurting and she never told us he was *that* good. Are you hurt, too, kid?"

Longarm replied with a muffled, "Nope." and hunkered down beside the man he'd gut-shot. There seemed no call to feel for a pulse and it was doubtful even a sawbones could have done much for the breed. So he just hunkered silent, the way Indians and folk reared around Indians were inclined to as they waited, polite, to be invited for supper or told to leave.

The breed Longarm suspected might be part Osage if he hailed from Kansas, seeing he was so mean, blew bloody bubbles as he asked his sidekick, he thought, where he'd shot that cock-sucking lawman.

Longarm softly replied, "High and low through the trunk, sideways as I flanked him up the slope."

The one that was still breathing, sort of, gasped, "That wasn't fair. You should have let him die slow, like me. You'll tell my Sally I made mention of her as I lay here, won't you, kid?"

Longarm quietly replied, "I will. What do you want me to tell Kansas Red?"

The dying man moaned, "You can tell her for me that she's stupid! I warned her they said Longarm was too big a boo for just the two of us. You heard her say he was just another man, no harder to fool than any other man she'd ever coped with."

"Where did we have this conversation with Kansas Red, Chief?" asked Longarm, knowing he was pushing his luck but hoping for the best.

It didn't work, the gut-shot breed groaned, "How come you ask such dumb questions at a time like this? You know full well where we were when she told us it was time to quit fucking around with Longarm and finish the game. Don't you pay any attention at all to where your own ass is planted, Jenkins?"

Then he opened one eye to peer up at Longarm in the tricky light and gasp, "Hey, you ain't Jenkins! What's going on? What happened to the kid?"

"I was helping him." Longarm replied, adding, "He asked me to take care of you, here, whilst he rode for a doc, see?"

The one they'd called Chief coughed, laughed bitterly, and replied in a suprisingly boyish tone, "God *damn* you're good, Longarm! I thought them were pistol shots I heard, up the slope. You got the kid, too, I take it?"

Longarm replied in as friendly a tone, "That's about the size of it. You wouldn't want to tell me where Kansas Red might be waiting on us all for word of the way things went?"

The breed murmured, wearily, "You shot me through the guts, not my brains. It's been nice talking to you, Longarm, but if you don't mind I've got to die, now."

But as a matter of fact, he was fibbing to the last. For 'though he never said another word it was a good three minutes before he stopped breathing and just lay there, like the useless garbage he and his pal up the slope were, now, seeing they'd lost.

Chapter 11

Longarm didn't want their side to know they'd lost, so he tidied up after the gunfight he'd just won. He backtracked along the trail to where they'd tethered their own mounts. He recognized both as stock he'd considered at that same livery in Manitou Springs. The center-fire saddles came with neither throw ropes, bedrolls, nor saddlebags. So he figured they'd been hired at the livery, too. The black-suited jaspers had followed him down from Denver by rail.

He knew the livery ponies would head back to their own stalls and feed bags on their own if he let 'em. But he didn't want anyone back in Manitou Springs to see 'em, and he knew the livery operators would have asked for deposits. So for now he led their hired mounts up the trail to where he'd tethered his own. Then he led all four ponies into the tall timber to tether them on the far side of that outcrop.

He broke out the folding camp-spade from his own possibles and dug a shallow double grave at the north base of the outcrop, where the sun might not beat down as hard and the drainage was fair. Then he dragged the two corpses down to repose them neatly after patting both down for evidence. He doubted they were really named Miller and Cooper, no matter what their Dodge City library cards said. But whilst any saddle tramp could get a library card just for the asking, Dodge City was in Kansas and the breed had admitted to knowing Kansas Red.

Longarm helped himself to their six-guns, derringers, pocket watches, and modest funds, seeing they'd have no further use for the same. He meant to hock their rifles as soon a he had the chance, too. Hocking guns instead of offering to sell them outright to a gunsmith brought in almost as much pocket jingle, and, since hocked guns would be held ninety days before being offered out front for sale, the deal could be Longarm's own little secret until then. If he hadn't caught Kansas Red within ninety days she was welcome to the information that her boys wouldn't be coming back.

As he covered the two of them with loose rock instead of soil, with a view to preserving them from critters but not rotting their faces off before he could send somebody out this way for them, Longarm could say he knew more about their gang, now, than he might have if they'd just let him the hell alone. He now knew that mysterious strawberry blonde with Irish features, according to Alvina Penn nee Lockwood, who'd seen her up close, was more than just a scout for the gang. The breed had admitted to taking orders from Kansas Red. That didn't mean she couldn't be the play-pretty of some male leader. The boss's wife was forever ordering the help around on many a spread. But however she fit in, Kansas Red was high on their totem pole, and giving orders to gun federal lawmen!

Longarm decided, "She's either crazy-mean or afraid I'm getting warm. I sure wish I knew what I was doing to worry them so. It sure feels as if I'm chasing my own tail like a confounded kitten who's smelled a rat but can't say where the fucker might be hiding!"

Once he figured he'd piled enough rock over the two cadavers, Longarm removed his hat, bowed his head, and said, "Well, if anybody's up yonder listening, I commend any souls these rascals might have had to whoever or whatever gives toad squat about such notions. For I have to get it on up the trail, now, and it's been nice talking to you."

He was glad he'd packed a coil of rope in one saddlebag, even though you didn't rope from a McClellan, because the long line came in handy for leading three ponies behind the paint he'd changed back to as he headed on up for Ute Pass.

He knew he'd never make it over the pass before sundown, now. But he didn't care because he'd changed his plans, now that he knew they were after him, personal. They called such plans, "Riding the owlhoot trail" because you were way less likely to meet other folk when you poked along in the dark and hid out during daylight hours. It was the slower but safer way to travel when the law, or outlaws, might be after you.

Longarm knew horses saw better in the dark than he did. So he wasn't as scared as some riders might have been, working his way over a mountain pass by starlight under a new moon. They forged on through the darkness, with him changing mounts more by feel than for sure, to ride slowly but surely into the tiny trail town of Florissant before midnight.

Florissant was French for flowery but you couldn't see much in the way of flowers or anything else as he reined in out front of a lamp-lit livery stable across from a general store cum saloon. The few business establishments in Florissant had to double in brass for any spare dimes that came their way, up their way.

Dealing first with the old fat lady running the livery, Longarm found her agreeable to helping the law and, as he'd hoped, in league with the livery outfits in Lake George to the west and Manitou Springs to the east in the management of trail stock. She said she'd be proud to see those mystery rider's hired mounts would be returned to Manitou Springs after they'd rested up at least seventy-two hours in her own paddock, out back. She refused to let Longarm pay for more than the watering and foddering of all four brutes whilst he mosied over to the brighter lights for some whistle-wetting and directions.

The younger gal serving behind the combined store counter and bar poured him a stein of hard cider, explaining their beer had gone bad in the half-empty keg with business so slow, and told him he'd almost overshot that survey trail he wanted to follow south to the S Bar P.

She said, "You'll miss the Hornbeck spread if you beeline across the ash flats toward the S Bar P, more to the southwest. But it's sort of late for them to coffee and cake a stranger in any case, and you said you were in a hurry."

Longarm said, "I am. If the Penn's homespread is going to cost me another twenty miles in the saddle, I'd best not shilly shally along the way."

The local gal, sort of weathered with mouse-colored hair gathered up in a bun, but otherwise not bad, warned, "You don't want to ride fast in the dark across them ash beds. They can make for tricky riding by broad day. Something awful happened down that way, one time."

She freshed his stein from her cider jug as she explained. "These college professors we had staying with us here, last summer said there used to be a string of lakes up the valley. Then mountains all about blew up and turned the valley into first a big old swamp and later the poor grazing you see down yonder today. The grass and low chaparral grows mostly where the earth below the ashy surface is solid, but not always. Bare gray stretches, or dead-flat fields of salt bush or cheat grass mean quicksand or at best boggy-going it's safer to ride around. Them professors dug up all sorts of flora and fauna turned to stone on them ash flats. Or *under* them ash flats, leastways. Sometimes you find petrified wood or the stone bones of outlandish critters, from bugs to what do you call them big-mouthed giant water hogs, hippodromes?"

Longam told her, "Hippopotamus is what they call the one in the Denver Zoo. I understand there used to be giant dragons traipsing around these mountains, back when they still lay flat and swampy. That surely must have been a sight. How do you reckon they drive stock in off the S Bar P to the south across such treacherous footing, ma'am?"

She said, "To begin with, they don't even try, after dark. When they can see what they're about they drive 'em along that well-blazed trail."

Longarm sipped thoughtfully and decided, "Well, I reckon you can keep a few head of cattle at a time to a trail that narrow. But I'd hate to try it with a fair-sized market herd."

The lady storekeeper-come-bartender shook her mouse-colored head to say, "Not cattle. Horses. The S Bar P is a big stud outfit, raising and breaking quality cow ponies. Didn't you know that?"

Longarm lost interest in her friendly ways and shapely figure as he replied, "I do now. We live and learn, once we manage to stay alive long enough. So I'd best settle up and be on my way, now, ma'am."

He rode on with his spare pony packing the salvaged weaponry for later. He was in a hurry. He wanted to get there before sunrise. But knowing he'd make better time on a blazed trail than trusting to his pony's night vision over treacherous riding, he beat back and forth through the starlit stirrup-high sage and cheat to find that easy to follow and doubtless way safer trail blazed across the ash flats by that government survey. They'd done a few things right, back in the Grant administration.

He couldn't make out a whole lot of fossils as he rode the owlhoot trail under a new moon, but he sensed he'd crossed to firmer parts of the South Park as high chaparral punctuated by aspen groves closed in from either side of the beaten path. He made better time, once he had fewer concerns about busting through to quicksand or worse, and, sure enough, he spied pinpoints of light, more than one, on the horizon to the south at around four thirty in the morning.

He heeled the chestnut he was riding faster, saying, "That's somebody up and about to make breakfast unless we're moving in on a haunted graveyard with the sky commencing to pearl to the east!"

By the time they were close enough to make out board-and-baton rooftops above the dotted line of lamp-lit windows the stars above were winking out against a cloudless, rosy sky. A yard dog commenced to bay as Longarm rode in. So he broke out his badge and pinned it to the front of his denim jacket lest they try to shoo him as a saddle tramp attracted by the coffee, bacon, and bisquits he could smell, now.

But he was greeted Christian before anybody could see him all that clear. A still-distant voice called out, "We ain't hiring, but you're in time for breakfast, stranger. Didn't they tell you in Florissant that we have enough help for now, down this way?"

Longarm waited until he was closer before he called back, "I ain't looking to hire on. I'm the law. U.S. Deputy Marshal Custis Long, down from Denver to see your boss lady, Miss Alvina. They told me over in Manitou Springs that I might find her out this way."

As he dismounted near the open doorway that swell

smell seemed to be coming from, he saw the hand calling out to him was a tall drink of water wearing a white shirt and tie but no hat above his own jeans and buscadero gun-rig. He was telling Longarm, "Miss Alvina ain't here at the moment, but we expect her back this morning. She took some of the boys out after a mustang stud that's been nickering brood mares off into the tall timber."

Longarm tethered the two ponies to the hitching rail along the back of the cookhouse, muttering half to himself, "I'm glad to hear she's been keeping herself so busy. I thought she was more worried than that."

The missing owner's obvious *segundo* came over to offer his hand and introduce himself as Sandy Bowmore before he asked in a mildly curious tone what Miss Alvina might have to worry about.

Longarm considered some before he responded. A paid up member of the W.C.T.U. who invited gents in plain English to fuck her sounded two-faced enough to keep things from her hired help, and few bragged to personal friends about horse thieves in the family.

So as he followed Bowmore inside, Longarm casually asked if they'd read anything in the papers about that shoot-out at the Kiowa Livery up Denver way.

The foreman waved Longarm to a seat at the long trestle table beyond the kitchen counters and swamping flat-top range as he casually replied that they only had the general store in Florissant save the Sunday editions of the *Rocky Mountain News* to be picked up with the mail when they sent a rider in for the same now and again.

Bowmore called out to the Chinee hovering over the pots and pans atop the kitchen range and the cook yelled back in a singsong tone of indignation, "Jesus Chlist who runny this fucky chuck hall, you lound-eyed plickhead? Betta you sit down, shut up, and let Fong do his fucky job!"

After they'd both chuckled fondly, Bowmore asked Longarm why they ought to care about a shoot-out up Denver way.

Longarm cautiously conceded, "A shady horse trader called MacLeod ran afoul of the law, trying to sell some stolen military mounts at the Kiowa Livery. Miss Alvina didn't tell you anything about that?"

Sandy Bowmore was either one hell of an actor or sincerely in the dark as he easily replied, "Not hardly. Why should she? I don't recall us having any dealing with a Denver horse trader named MacLeod. That would be a Scotch name, wouldn't it?"

The fuming Oriental cook sent a shy Indian he'd been hiding to the table with their mugs of Arbuckle and earthenware plates, big plates, of bacon and biscuits. Cowhands worked for a dollar a day and up with found, or room and board when they weren't out on the range. Longarm had ridden for outfits that fed smaller portions, on tin plates instead of earthenware decent enough for a chili parlor. He chose his words carefully as he replied, "MacLeod said it was. Correct me if I'm wrong, but ain't Bowmore a Scotch name, too?"

The lean *segundo* nodded without hesitation and replied, "Part of Clan MacDonald of the Islands. That's how I knew MacLeod was another Highland name."

He helped himself to some bacon and biscuits, washed it down with black coffee as Longarm went through the same motions, and added in a sarcastic tone, "For the record, the MacDonalds and MacLeods were at feud in the old country and I ride for a boss lady with a Welsh name."

Longarm said, "I think her maiden name, Lockwood, would be English. Might you know her kid brother, Edward Lockwood, Sandy?"

The *segundo*, who doubtless had the power to hire and fire on the S Bar P, made a wry face but kept his voice polite as he said, "Not that well. He tried his hand at wrangling for Miss Alvina the summer he . . . left college. He didn't seem to have a calling for working with ponies."

Longarm cautiously asked, "Do tell? I heard he's been known to deal in horseflesh up around Denver, now and again. Are you sure his big sister never mentioned anything about her kid brother and a fancy palomino he . . . had for sale?"

And once again Longarm felt the foreman of Alvina Penn nee Lockwood's stud spread was telling the simple truth when he answered, simply, "Not a word. I hadn't heard a thing about her kid brother dealing in horseflesh, too. I honestly didn't think he had it in him. Albeit just between you, me, and nobody else, I wouldn't be surprised to hear the lazy little shit had *stole* a horse!"

Chapter 12

It was wrong to speak ill of the dead and dumb to deal your cards faceup when you didn't have to. So Longarm didn't say what he had to talk to their boss lady about, and after they ate Sandy Bowmore showed Longarm around the S Bar P's homespread.

Like most stock operations west of say Longitude 100°, the S Bar P consisted of a proven tax-paying homestead claim or a well watered quarter section surrounded by public land that wasn't worth grazing if you didn't control the water.

Bowmore explained and Longarm believed that the late Sid Penn had filed on other quarter sections scattered along the west slopes of the Front Range in the names of kith and kin who'd then sold out to him, fee simple, once their five-year improvement provisions were up and the homesteads had become private land to have and to hold or sell cheap to a pal.

Unlike cows that ranged in big circles around salt blocks and water, or sheep and goats as had to be watched constant by a herder and at least one good dog, horses had minds of their own and they'd run off to turn mustang if you let 'em. So whilst the main house, bunkhouse, chuck house, workshops, storage sheds, and Bowmore's own separate office and quarters were set up in the usual fortlike square, surrounded by the usual corrals, kitchen gardens, and such, they'd strung pole fences to enclose pastures and paddocks all the way out to the limits of their government claim, to feed the stock hay cut on open range beyond.

As they circled afoot, Longarm saw some enclosures were lying empty and fallow to let the sod recover, whilst others held mostly young and frisky stock to romp strong across plenty of space, or breeding stock with the mares and studs penned separate, save for the noisy nickering-and-kicking times they were allowed to cuddle closer.

Longarm failed to spot any brands reading 808 or any of the other easy ways to run the federal US. Fewer than half the ponies he saw were that shade of bay the military prefered, unless it was gray for the army bands, and most were a tad runty by cavalry standards. So he asked and Bowmore told him most cattle outfits preferred paints or buckskins, no more than fourteen hands at the withers. Longarm knew why. The *segundo* still told him a mount with shorter forelegs could zig-zag better after a bawling calf whilst most young cowhands admired distinctive riding stock and, seeing they had to ride a different one every day, flashy hides made it easier for the wrangler to keep the remuda rotating in order.

By now the sun was hanging above the Front Range to their east and Bowmore seemed a tad concerned. Then a kid on a jug-headed paint rode in to tell them Miss Alvina and the others had that rogue mustang stud boxed in a blind canyon with some S Bar P mares and wanted him to come back with some sandwiches, seeing they figured to take a spell.

Longarm didn't ask why. He'd mustanged, himself, in his time. While the Chinee rustled up some trail grub,

102

Longarm asked and Bowmore loaned him a fresh mount to ride back to the hunting party with the kid.

The errand boy had naturally switched his saddle and bridle to a fresh roan. Longarm had taken Bowmore's word about a chunky cordovan with a white blaze. It was only in kids books about black beauties that the same horse could carry anyone for hours on end, like it ran on steam like a four-legged locomotive.

Mounted on fresh ponies, Longarm and the kid headed south at a lope. The kid said Miss Alvina had allowed she was hungry. The way they kept her spread for her, up here, when she spent most of her time down in a fresh-painted and well-staffed mansion in Manitou Springs, bespoke a boss lady her help paid attention to. It seemed hardly likely the soft, sweet taffy blonde had ever asked Sandy Bowmore, right out, to fuck her.

As the kid had promised, it wasn't far south along the western aprons, of the Front Range, where aspen, alder, and cottonwood sprouted from rocky scree along the edges of the sage and grass flats, that they came upon a cluster of tethered cow ponies with another kid in attendance.

He pointed east and told them the others had decided to pussyfoot in and see if they couldn't pick off that worthless wild stud without shooting any of the mares he'd nickered off.

Longarm and the kid dismounted. Longarm took his own saddle gun. The kid packed that feed sack of paper-wrapped sandwiches as they headed on up the dry gravel bed of a sometimes torrent that had carved a sort of canyon down from higher ground.

It was the sort of canyon you got in the more wooded high country to the northeast of the dramatic canyon-lands to the southwest. The walls rose less steep and bare. But a forty-five degree slope covered with sticker-brush could discourage any critter less Alpine than a mountain goat or bighorn, so Longarm saw what the plan was as he and the kid legged it up the steep enough going along the gravel bed of the overgrown gully.

They heard a not-too-distant rifle shot and put their backs into it to swing a bend and then, up ahead, they spied four others on foot, one in a tan whipcord riding habit, standing in a circle around the black fallen figure of a good-sized horse.

The kid chortled, "Hot damn! They got him!" Kids were always saying things like that. As the two of them moved closer, Longarm saw that gal in the riding habit had her taffy blonde hair pinned up in a bun above her bowed bare head. Her Spanish hat hung down her back on a braided leather chin-thong. She was holding a Springfield .45-70 down at her side. As they moved closer, Longarm could see she was crying. When they were close enough they heard her sobbing, "You big beautiful fool, you should have listened to your elders and just stayed away from our kind entire! You could have lived out your life as free as the wind with all the wild wives you could service, but you had to get greedy and now you're dead and, Lord, you sure were some horse!"

Longarm wasn't looking forward to telling a gal that sentimental about dead horses that her brother was dead, too. But he had to, so he took off his hat as the kid hailed them and she turned to face them with a curious smile.

Longarm had never locked eyes with the lady before in his life.

After that her eyes were indeed chocolate brown, her hair was taffy blonde, and he reckoned that under that healthy tan her hide might be more vanilla ice cream in tone. So Longarm called out, "I'm from the U.S. Marshal's office up to Denver, ma'am. They sent me down here to call on Miss Alvina Penn nee Lockwood. I take it you'd be her sister?"

The petite taffy blonde who'd just shot a big black horse shook her totally strange but just as pretty head to reply, "I don't have any sister. I'm Alvina Penn. Is this about my brother, Edward? I heard he was in trouble again."

Longarm put his hat back on to give himself time to think, once he'd allowed that was about the size of it.

The Widow Penn, the real Widow Penn, it appeared, suggested they talk in private and turned on one boot heel, like a lady used to having her own way. So Longarm followed as she led the way further up the bed of the canyon. As they moved out of earshot of the others, Longarm saw scattered mares, peeking out of the bushes at them like kids who'd been playing hide-and-seek, wondering what happened next, now that the game seemed over.

The strange taffy blonde paused when she came to a rock worth bracing one booted foot on as she turned to face him. Before he could say anything she said, "I warned Edward the last time he stole a horse that I'd never bail him out again. He has to learn that stealing horses is a serious offense in Colorado."

Longarm nodded and agreed, "Capital, as a matter of fact."

She grimaced and said, "Pooh, you know I'll never let them hang him. I fear he's banking on our lawyer getting him out on appeal. For nobody sees through a bluff like a dedicated black sheep with well-off relations. How far along might his case be, now, and how come the U.S. Marshal's office is interested in the first place?"

Longarm took a deep breath, let half of it out to keep his voice dead level and gently said, "Your brother's dead, ma'am. Murdered, we suspect, by outlaws wanted for stealing government stock."

He was braced to grab for her if she fainted. But she just swayed a mite like she'd been punched but wasn't going to let it show. She took some deep breaths of her own, then she calmly asked for the whole sad story.

By the time Longarm finished she was seated on that rock with Longarm hunkered nearby. He could see, now, why her kid brother and others had described her as sort of imperious. But he liked a woman who could think whilst she was asking questions. She said she doubted her kid brother had ever had enough ambition to ride with a gang. He'd hated to take orders or even suggestions and couldn't seem to keep his mind on any chores he'd agreed to. She said, when they'd been little, she'd had to finish splitting the supper stove-wood out back, most of the time, because Edward had been inclined to drop the ax and chase after butterflies or grasshoppers.

Longarm nodded soberly and said, "He spoke highly of you, the few times I spoke with him, ma'am. He said he'd *sold* stray ponies he'd sort of found to Hoss MacLeod. He never said he'd ridden with MacLeod's gang."

The real Alvina said, "I didn't know that slippery dealer *had* any gang. I've heard other bad things about him, of course. Everyone in the business this close to the Denver stockshows has heard about Hoss MacLeod. But Mister MacLeod is, or was, a dealer more interested in *buying* than *selling* around the Denver yards. It was my understanding he bought cheap and sold dear, shipping ponies by rail up to the fresh north ranges where new cattle spreads are sprouting and a good cowpony can sell for a hundred dollars or more."

Longarm stared down at the sun-baked gravel to muse, half to himself, "MacLeod *said*, as he lay dying, he'd come there that evening to bid on those military bays, not to sell them. But that other gal who said she was you told us MacLeod had approached her with an offer to *sell*. Makes you wonder, don't it?"

To which she replied without hesitation, "No it doesn't. She wasn't telling the truth when she said she was me. Why couldn't she have been lying when she said she'd been offered stock she'd told Mister MacLeod she was selling?"

Longarm nodded thoughtfully, but asked, "Why indeed? She told me the mysterious Kansas Red had approached her about them stolen bays. Hoss MacLeod said he'd thought Kansas Red's gang would be there to *sell* the same ponies. So somebody was surely fibbing, but to what end?"

The horse-breeding gal sounded sure as she replied, "To put MacLeod out of business, as they did! Don't you see how those scheming women did the poor little toad in? That redhead and her riders stole those military mounts and hid them somewhere around the stockyard sprawl near the railroad complex. Then that blonde one approached you, knowing it was safe to say she was me because—"

"How?" Longarm cut in, explaining, "She and her own pals had to know you wouldn't come running to bail your kid brother out before they could sweep MacLeod and your kid brother off the board. Don't that mean they have pals of your own, or folk you take for pals, keeping an eye on you, down this way?"

She shrugged and said, "They'd only need one spy, watching the railroad stop near that Western Union office in Manitou Springs. A horse thief by definition is inclined to accept greater risks than my boarding a train for Denver while that snip who'd bleached her hair to match mine was having her wicked way with you!"

"She's a natural taffy blonde," Longarm insisted, not going further into just how wicked that other Alvina had acted.

The real Alvina shrugged and said, "Be that as it may,

she pretended to be me, confounded by the approaches of a known crook, and so you and those other men naturally believed her, went along with the chance she offered to entrap a thief with hot horseflesh to sell, and put a rival out of business when the confused MacLeod bunch went down in a blinding haze of gunsmoke. She and that redhead must still be laughing at you!"

Longarm soberly replied, "Some ladies do seem to find us menfolk comical. Are you suggesting the Kansas Red gang, for lack of a better handle to call 'em, just took advantage of your kid brother's arrest on an unrelated charge to take over MacLeod's bigger operations around the Denver stockyards, ma'am?"

She said, "I have to get up to Denver to see about Edward's proper burial. I don't know why those lying thieves wanted you lawmen to gun down Hoss MacLeod. I don't care. I only want to know who gunned my brother and what you mean to do about it!"

He told her, honestly, "I'm sure we're talking about the same crooks with the same or similar motives, Miss Alvina. They knew Hoss MacLeod was dead when they shot your brother on the streets of Denver. So they must have thought he knew something. They must have feared he'd told me what he knew because they tried to gun me, just the other side of Ute Pass, before I could get here."

She shrugged and said, "I've no idea what Edward might have known about them. We haven't been close since the last time he was arrested. But he was my brother, and I have to do right by him, so I'd better get cracking."

Longarm said, "It's your Christian duty, ma'am. But with your kind permit I mean to escort you, close and personal, all the way up to the capitol, and you'd best pack your own sidearm aboard the train. Them killers must think Edward told me something. If he had, I've just had time to pass it on to you and they have no way of knowing for certain whether you're headed north for a funeral or an appearance before a federal grand jury, see?"

She nodded, grimly and said, "I do. Let's not say anything about this to my riders. It's nobody's beeswax but my own and they have to have somebody spying on me for that other blonde to have known so much about me."

Longarm started to point out that it wouldn't take much acting ability to impersonate a lady he'd never heard tell of before she approached him up Denver way.

Then the real Alvina calmly murmured, "Since we're going to be in one another's company on the trail and by rail for some time, we'd better get it straight that you're not to get ideas whilst we're alone. When I want to fuck a man I tell him so. I don't hold with simpering smiles and flirty remarks when I've better things to do, hear?"

He'd heard. So had that other taffy blonde, it appeared. He had to wonder whether she'd have gone all the way with her impersonation at the Tremont House if he'd taken her up on it.

Chapter 13

They rode in to Florissant before sundown, had a full meal whilst their mounts rested some, and then, mindful of some unknown enemy with other dry gulchers possibly posted along the trail, rode by night over the pass and down as far as Woodland Park before dawn, where the real Alvina was naturally known as one of the bigger frogs in their little pond. So they had no trouble leaving all their ponies in the care of her pals at the local livery and hopping the narrow guage short-line on to Colorado Springs, where they caught a few hours' sleep in separate hotel rooms before Longarm wired a progress report ahead and wrangled them a free ride north in the main line freight caboose.

They got in around quitting time, for most folk, and caught a hansom cab to the Federal Building where, as Longarm had told the worried gal, Marshal Billy Vail was always the last big shot to leave for the day.

It took some backing and filling for the gruffly courteous older lawman to tumble to the fact that Longarm wasn't introducing him to the same Alvina Penn nee Lockwood they'd been talking about when Vail had sent him south to break the news to her about her brother.

With Vail behind the desk and Alvina seated in the single horsehair-padded leather chair provided, Longarm stood behind it as he explained, "Miss Alvina, here, wasn't the Miss Alvina who told us she'd been approached by the late Hoss MacLeod to bid on those purloined ponies from Camp Weld."

"Horses," the taffy blonde cut in, with some authority.

She added, "A pony is any saddle mount standing less than fourteen hands at the withers. Neither the Army nor State Remount services will consider a mount less than fourteen hands or better, making it a horse and not a pony!"

"Unless it's a gelding or a mare tall enough for the remount buyers." Longarm was unable to resist.

She sniffed and said, "If you can put a saddle or a horse collar on it, I can sell you either. I know everyone else calls any saddle bronc you chase cattle on a cow pony and the reporters never mount our Indian Fighting Army aboard mares or, perish the thought, mules. But those of us in horse trading describe our wares with nicety and you did say Hoss MacLeod was a horse trader, didn't you?"

Vail grimaced and said, "There's some differance of opinion about that, over to the stockyards, ma'am. Me and my other deputies have been scouting the slippery Scotchman's backtrail whilst the two of you have been working your way back up here. At the risk of sounding like a know-it-all, I've already given the matter of that stolen military stock a heap of thought."

He cocked a quizzical brow at Longarm, who shrugged and said, "Horse thieves by definition steal horses, and we already discussed the lighter sentences you get for stealing horses from Uncle Sam."

Vail grimaced some more and said, "Maybe. Gossip around the stockyards and some of the seedier saloons west of Larimer confirms some of what MacLeod told you as he lay dying. He was likely at the Kiowa Livery to bid on them bays from Camp Weld. Not to sell them, as that other Miss Alvina suggested."

Longarm pointed out, "She never suggested it, Boss. She told me right out that she was the horse-trading Widow Penn, here, and that Hoss MacLeod had approached her with a view to unloading military stock he admitted were stolen."

Then he frowned thoughtfully and added, "We now know she was fibbing about other matters and the dying MacLeod told me he'd been invited to meet another gal entire there, that night, to bid on stolen stock *she* had for sale!"

Vail nodded and said, "I vote we buy his tale of woe as the lesser of two likely lies. Whilst you were out in the field we had no trouble finding the stud farm Hoss MacLeod owned and operated out by Arvada. We found a couple of stolen carriage horses and another saddle mount Hoss never aquired from its proper owner, mixed in with scrub stock he was likely holding in his corrals to confound the issue. We found no military bays at all, but some bitty kids from a nearby orphan home, playing hide and go seek in some second growth sticker-brush we suspect MacLeod planted around his spread on purpose, recalled some right handsome chargers, as kids describe cavaly mounts standing a hand or more taller than the uncurried scrub stock milling with 'em in the same corral."

"But you say they're not out there, now?" Longarm brightened, trying not to dwell too much on the Arvada Orphan Asylum ahead of time.

Billy Vail said, "The kids Goldman and Ryan canvassed said you never saw any of them frisky chargers out back of MacLeod's place all that long. Never more than a day or so. Then nothing but the same scrub stock they never seemed to hire out or sell until, sure enough, they'd peek out of the sticker-brush one morning to spy another six or eight high-spirited chargers, like you see more often in books, with princes or armored knights mounted up on 'em."

Alvina decided, "That slippery dealer you say my brother dealt with must have had a ready market for that sort of stock. But, for the life of me, I can't think of anywhere in Colorado you could unload that many military mounts on anyone but the military!"

Vail said, "We figure MacLeod had to be reselling to a middleman who drives them along the owlhoot trail to the new cattle spreads springing up in the Powder River Country, now that the buffalo and Mister Lo, The Poor Indian, ain't hogging all that yummy buffalo grass."

"To what end?" she objected, pointing out in that same tone of authority, "You don't work cattle on cavalry mounts. Even if they were built for dodging and weaving instead of speed and endurance, you have to *train* any mount as a cowpony before you can *work* cows with it! Try to rope a calf at full gallop from a cavalry mount and, if you're lucky, you'll never come close to roping it because, if you do, the calf will surely spill you and your poor military mount when it hits the end of any tied down throw-rope at a dead run!"

Longarm smiled fondly down at the part in her taffy hair to remark to his boss, "The little lady knows a thing or two about the equine species and I'd say she's on to something we may have overlooked about the market for horseflesh up Wyoming way. When you study on the cattle industry, it's *possible* to get by with untrained riding stock for kid jobs such as tailing the herd or loping in to the railroad stop for the recent beef prices. But wouldn't a green hand mounted on a big old bay branded 808 attract at least some local gossip?"

Vail shrugged and said, "Goldman suggested Ute

medicine men might be in the market for what them kids call chargers. Lots of heap big pow-wows going on, west of the divide, with the B.I.A. fixing to move even more Ute out to the Great Basin. Medicine man sacrificing a noteworthy cavalry steed, as Ute are inclined to—"

"That won't work," Longarm cut in, explaining, "Chief Colorow is down on his fat knee this summer, pleading with his Great White Father for peace whilst Governor Pitkin and the Colorado Guard are patrolling both banks of the White River for any Ute kid wearing paint or shaking rattle one. The bigger boys of the Ute nation are gathered over in their sacred Uncomphagre valley, under constant military observation. How many head of stolen military stock would you care to run way out yonder to make blood medicine and, even assuming religious frenzy, where would those formerly wild Indians get enough money to make such a transaction worth half the risk?"

Alvina rose to her feet, declaring, "While you gentlemen discuss livestock I've no real interest in, my poor wayward brother lies on ice, I hope, at the county morgue. So with our permission, I'll be on my way to the Forsythe Funeral Home to arrange a decent burial for our poor black sheep."

But Vail said, "You don't have my permit, Miss Alvina. I'm taking you home with me for the night. Don't get excited and don't get upset. My wife will be proud to fix you up with a warm supper and a soft bed in the guest room."

"But my brother can't spend another night on a cold marble slab!" she protested.

"Galvinized iron, Miss Alvina." Longarm gently corrected, going on to explain, "You're right about them being cold. It's better that way. But they keep the bodies on big steel trays, coated with zinc lest they rust. I suspect what Marshal Vail is worried about would be them

114

other bodies I wired about from Colorado Springs. Buried shallow up near Ute Pass."

Vail nodded grimly and agreed, "That's about the size of it, ma'am. They haven't tried for anyone else on our side since they gunned your brother to keep him quiet. So I reckon they're worried your brother might have told Custis something and, since he's had plenty of time to tell you, and since it could have been a family secret to begin with, you ain't about to show your pretty face on the nigh deserted streets of downtown Denver after dark."

Longarm could sense her chagrin. So he volunteered, "I could drop by that funeral home this evening and ask them to send someone up to the Vail house to talk to you, Miss Alvina."

Vail shook his head to say, "Don't want either of you children out of the house until we figure out who might be after either one of you, and how come. I can send someone else to fetch the undertaker for this little lady. You'd best hole up here or up to my place, Custis. Anybody knowing they're after such a famous lawman could know you usually turn in alone at that rooming house across Cherry Creek."

Longarm had to look away. He knew that Billy Vail knew of another place he often turned in, just down Sherman from the Vail house. For the marshal's old lady had been after the both of them for the gossip she'd heard about that across her backyard fence.

Lest Longarm fail to follow his drift, Vail added, "We wouldn't want them shooting up your rooming house or any other innocent bystanders, would we, old son?"

Longarm tersely replied, "Wasn't planning on getting too close to . . . any innocent bystanders, this evening. But I can't cut for sign up to your place or along the deserted corridors around here after sundown. I'm likely as dangerous as they are, awake and on the prod on my feet. So I figured I'd drift through the seamier underbelly of Denver near the stockyards and chew some fat with some of my own informants. Them orphans playing around MacLeod's stud farm near Arvada can't be the only ones who'd admire a well curried military mount in unsusual company."

Vail said, "I don't want you pestering anybody at that Arvada Orphan Asylum, either. That's an order."

So the Vails had heard gossip about him and the head mistress out to the Arvada Orphan Asylum, had they? A lot *they* knew.

Longarm stiffly assured his boss, "I wasn't planning on riding clear over to Arvada. You just told me how you and the boys canvassed those orphans and recovered no federal stock at MacLeod's spread out yonder."

Alvina Penn nee Lockwood hadn't been following their veiled conversation, but that hadn't kept her from thinking.

She said, "I seem to be missing something. Wouldn't Custis, here, have already told you anything my poor brother might have told him? Why would they have tried to shoot him this side of Ute Pass, before he could ever talk to me if they were afraid *I* might tell him something? Wouldn't it have made more sense for them to send those gunslicks after me in the first place? Neither I nor anybody riding for me would have been on guard and, even if we had been, my foreman, Sandy, wouldn't be half as risky to tangle with as a lawman with so many notches in his gun!"

Longarm modestly pointed out, "Nobody but fool kids trying to look mean ever cut notches in their gun grips, Miss Alvina. But I do see what you mean and it cheers me some to suspect it might be me and me alone they were after."

"How come?" demanded Billy Vail, insisting, "You've had plenty of time to pass on any secrets Edward Lockwood might have told you. So why would they expect you to be holding something back on us for later?"

Longarm shrugged and said, "If I knew I'd never hold it back on you. I'll be switched with snakes if I can come up with an educated guess!"

The dead Lockwood's sister suggested, "What if they're afraid my brother told you who that horrid Kansas Red really was, and where you might be able to find her between raids?"

Longarm shook his head wearily and replied, "We'd have arrested her by now and they have to know that. Ditto the true identities of any of the rest of her gang. There ain't a lawman in these parts who hasn't figured out by this time how Kansas Red and her gang suckered a rival horse thief called Hoss MacLeod into the stakeout they invited the law to partake in. Both Hoss MacLeod and the law were used and abused by a mighty sneaky bunch. But that can't be a secret they were hoping to keep from us."

Billy Vail decided, "They were out to eliminate a rival and they done it. Going over your report on the death of Edward Lockwood—Sorry, Miss Alvina, I read how he'd confessed to you that he'd unloaded some few saddle broncs, albeit never any military mounts, on Hoss MacLeod. He'd told you just before he was caught in the crossfire, he'd heard tell of Kansas Red but didn't know her. So the last question before the house would be what he might have told you about where Hoss MacLeod sent hot horseflesh, *any* hot horseflesh, from that stud farm out Arvada way!"

Alvina asked, "What makes you think Edward was caught in cross fire? How can we be certain he wasn't the target to begin with?"

Vail said, "Nothing's certain but death and taxes, ma'am. But after they fired on your brother and Custis, here, they fired on Custis some more on his way to fetch you. So add it up."

Longarm said, "They could have been after either one of us. I mean to ask them when I catch them. Meanwhile the three of us are only talking in circles and I know others, closer to the stockyards, who might know some straighter answers."

So Vail agreed and the three of them parted friendly on the granite steps out front, with Vail and Alvina headed east toward his house up on Capitol Hill and Longarm ambling west in the gloaming light, hugging the shadows some and covering the deserted sidewalks behind him with a little help from the reflective glass of darkened downtown shops until he was sure nobody was trailing him, at the moment.

Then he cut through an alley to make double certain before he headed for the quarters of Miss Morgana Floyd, the head mistress riding hard on all those kids out to the Arvada Orphan Asylum.

He'd told Billy Vail he wasn't going all the way out to the village of Arvada and he hadn't been fibbing, as soon as you studied on it. For at this hour all those orphans would be tucked in bed, watched over by a skeleton night crew, whilst the petite brunette head mistress of the whole shebang would be bedded down near the Denver County Morgue and, with any luck, feeling sort of lonesome in the gathering dusk.

Chapter 14

Calling on a possible witness in the line of duty, once you studied on it, Longarm found the mighty pretty but sort of shy-looking Morgana had turned in early with a good book. For as she'd confessed when first they'd met, aboard that runaway streetcar on the slope of Capitol Hill, it was tough to meet men whilst herding orphans around in a starched poplin uniform and they'd have never met at all had Longarm not been in the process of saving her and all those screaming kids when the horse-drawn streetcar they'd boarded for a summer outing had gone careening lickey split down the grade.

But, being a woman, even as she stood there in her doorway dressed for bed in a cotton shimmy shirt under her open kimono, breathing hard, Morgana had to demand what had happened to that Chinee waitress they'd told her he'd been sparking.

Longarm wearily assured her, "I ain't been visiting with any other gals in Denver for a coon's age! I just got in from a field mission down by Pikes Peak and don't you want to hear about it?"

That worked. She sighed and said, "This better be good. You can tell me all about it, you lying rascal, whilst I whip us up some scrambled eggs."

So he hung up his hat and gunrig to sit at her kitchen table as she poked the banked coals of her small range aflame and by the time he'd gotten to that shootout near Ute Pass he had her interested enough to tell him, "Some of your junior deputies were out to the orphanage, asking some of our older charges about a nearby stud farm. Do you suspect the owner was tied in with the outlaws who were out to kill you?"

To which Longarm could only reply, "I don't know yet. We've asked the sheriff of El Paso County to send a buckboard up from Colorado Springs to recover them bodies. If they turn out to be wanted anywheres, the sheriff is welcome to the bounties. If they ain't, I got to pay from my own pocket for a proper burial with minimum fuss."

Morgana put a coffeepot and cast-iron spider on her range to heat up as she remarked, "That hardly seems fair, Custis. How come *you're* expected to bear the cost?"

He shrugged and said, "Somebody has to and I'm the one who shot 'em. There's some logic to the firm but fair federal regulations. When any lawman catches up with an outlaw out in the middle of nowheres it's a big temptation to drop him where you find him and save the bother of bringing him back alive. So they pay you a few cents a mile and pocket change for doing it the hard way and stick you with the disposal of the body if they have to take your word that you just had to shoot him. It could be worse. They could make you stand trial every time you had to gun an outlaw."

Morgana made a face and said, "Heavens! I'd never want to carry a badge if they were *that* strict!"

As she picked up a jar of bacon drippings from a nearby windowsill, Longarm laconically explained, "That's doubtless why they split the difference the way they do. But to answer your first question, we're fairly sure they'll turn out to be *somebody*. Once we have a handle on who they might have been we'll be in better shape to guess who they were riding for. I'll be mighty surprised if they were out to avenge Hoss MacLeod, albeit that's possible. It's more likely they were sent by the same gang that Kansas Red rides with. How old and how reliable are those kids who reported those handsome bay military mounts in Hoss MacLeod's corrals, Miss Morgana?"

As she glopped some congealed bacon drippings in the spider, Morgana coyly replied, "You didn't call me 'miss' the last time you were here, you naughty boy. Those ten-year-olds your junior deputies questioned were being naughty, too. Arvada's not that big a town and they did have my permission to leave the confines of our orphanage to play tag or hide-and-seek, but that stud farm was way over on the far side of Arvada and they were spying on a *horse thief*!"

Longarm said, "I was inclined to peek in windows when I was ten, ah, honey. It's an awkward time to kill time in. You're getting on for kid games and ain't figured out why the grown folks are acting so odd around one another, yet."

As she got some fresh eggs from her corner icebox, Morgana blushed a mite and murmured, "You hadn't learned to pleasure yourself by the time you were *ten*? Poor baby, it's small wonder you grew up to be so horny! I questioned those boys, myself, after your friends were done with them. Not about masturbation. About those cavalry horses they said they saw. I don't think they made anything up."

As she busted eggs on the edge of the sizzling spider Longarm told her, "Neither do I. The newspaper accounts of the shoot-out at the Kiowa Livery never described the riding stock MacLeod had either come to buy

121

or sell. I reckon ten-year-old boys know a big bay from a smaller cowpony. The ones your charges spotted in MacLeod's corral would have been from earlier raids on military remudas. I doubt the ones run off from Camp Weld ever got that far west. MacLeod told me he'd come to bid on them as he lay dying and I've started to buy his sad story. He was set up for a fall by rivals. Two of which would seem to have been women of considerable perfidity. MacLeod said the strawberry blonde they call Kansas Red invited him to join her at the Kiowa Livery that evening to look over horses *she* had for sale. At about the same time a taffy blonde pretending to be a more honest horse trader approached *me* with an invite to the same party. I've yet to match wits with Kansas Red, but if she fibs half as slick as her taffy-blonde pard I can see how they slickered poor old Hoss MacLeod. They had us slickered total. The one I talked to looked nothing like the real Widow Penn, up close and personal. But she fit the other lady's overall description, save for being paler and a tad softer looking."

Morgana scrambled the eggs harder than she really needed to as she observed in a withering tone, "Trust you to know just how soft the two of them were, you brute, and if I had any willpower I'd throw you out this minute!"

Longarm calmly replied, "I never got to feel up either of 'em, as a matter of fact. But, for the record, the crooked one offered, and yet I remained true to you . . . all. The impersonating blonde knew all about the real Widow Penn's family and background, but either had her morals wrong or they'd told how much a lawman hates to arrest a gal he'd known in the biblical sense."

"Maybe she just liked you," Morgana suggested as she filled their plates and poured two cups of boiling water with unnecessary roughness. Then she plopped two tea bags in the cups and sat down across from him, looking cross.

Longarm reached across the table to pat her wrist, soothing, "I said I never took her up on it. Do you reckon it's possible that's why she sent those gunslicks after me as I rode off to leave her pure? They do say hell hath no fury like a woman scorned and it's possible some mighty mean gals have wound up ordering a gang of horse thieves about."

Morgana was intelligent as well as a tad possessive. So she demured, "One bandit queen I'll buy. Not two. For the same reason you never find two queen bees in the same hive."

He dug into the scrambled eggs, surprised by how hungry he'd gotten since that early supper of mulligan stew aboard that caboose with another lady entire. He was getting another erection, come to study back on all that chaste time he'd spent with old Alvina.

But it was early and they hadn't finished eating, so he mused, half to himself, "Oh, I dunno, that other redhead, the Princess of Wales, is said to put up with the likes of Miss Lily Langtry and she's almost a queen. I mean the Princess of Wales is almost a queen. Lily Langtry will never make it past play-pretty."

Morgana said, "My point, exactly. Princess Alex may be just as happy to let some other poor girl pleasure that fat slob she's stuck with if she ever hopes to be Queen of England. But she doesn't share a lick of power or a square foot of her palace with any of her husband's love toys. So one or the other of those outlaw girls you've mentioned has to be the real boss, or the favorite of the real boss, right?"

Longarm shrugged and replied, "What if one gal is the leader and the other is *her* love toy? They do say lezzy gals can act mannish and strong willed."

Morgana demurely asked, "Didn't you just say the taffy blonde tried to fuck you, dear?"

Longarm sighed wistfully and truthfully replied, "She sure acted as if she wanted to. But some lezzy gals can enjoy life both ways and, even when they don't, a whole lot of parlor-house gals are secret lezzies who don't cotton to men at all."

He washed down some scrambled eggs with her weak tea and added with a grimace of distaste, "I've yet to decide whether a gal who sells her body to a gent she finds repulsive or a gal who likes it but makes her lovers pay for it would have to feel the most unhappy with herself."

Morgana sighed and said, "I just wish I could say no! But you know I can't, so, all right, how long do you mean to stay, this time?"

Longarm polished off the last of his eggs to give himself time to choose his words before he told her, "I can't say. I don't know how long I'll be here in Denver. Me and my sidekicks may or may not get a line on where in thunder Hoss MacLeod sent all them stolen military mounts. Deputy Goldman likes the far side of the divide, to be used as medicine sacrifices. I don't buy that notion. My boss, Billy Vail, has 'em headed north to them new cattle spreads along the Powder River. But a lady who raises and busts broncs to various purposes insists a full-sized horse-trained Cavalry Style would make too poor a cowpony to be worth running government brands and moving them that far, to sell at any price you could ask a boss wrangler with a lick of sense."

She said to leave the dishes where they were as she rose to take him by the hand and lead him from the table, idly asking how one got a whole lot of hot horseflesh from Arvada, Colorado, to the Powder River country of Wyoming Territory.

As she led him the short way to her feather bed he

124

told her they were working on whether Hoss MacLeod had been sneaking stolen stock out to cooler climes by rail or by the owlhoot trail. Both had advantages and neither could hope to totally avoid some witness who'd been left out of the payoffs coming forward. Before he could get to MacLeod's exact methods being moot, since a new bunch had apparently taken over his horse trading for fun and profit, they were in bed together, having a whole lot of fun that wasn't costing either of them a dime.

"Oh, Custis, you're such an animal and I'm so glad!" She was purring, once they'd gotten a frantic first orgasm and all their duds out of the way. He felt no call to comment on her animal nature as she thrust her firm, shapely rump up by lamplight, dog style, even though she'd been the one to suggest the position.

As he stood there with his bare feet spread on her braided-rag rug, gazing fondly down at the view as he grasped a hip bone in either palm to slide her on and off his raging erection like a tight wet glove, he could see how come fat Princes of Wales with pretty red-headed wives at home might enjoy a change of pace with say a sultry brunette actress.

The handsome Princess of Wales was a Danish red-head, built tall and willowsome next to the part French Lily Langtry from the Channel Isle of Jersey. Being a man, his ownself, Longarm doubted like hell that his nibs of Wales wasn't screwing his wife and mistress, or mistresses, in turn. He'd once worked a murder case where the young mistress of a federal judge had been outraged to discover he'd been sleeping with his wife on rare occasions. After helpings of steak and mashed potatoes, a bowl of clam chowder or some noodles and dumplings really hit the spot. So as he was admiring the sight of his love-slicked shaft sliding in and out of this petite brunette he naturally compared the vision with that of the softer and wider bottomed brown-haired widow up on Sherman Street and, whilst he was at it, he'd ridden the Utah Pass Trail behind that other widow long enough to have a pretty fair notion what *her* bare ass might look like under these same conditions.

"Good heavens, you're so *passionate* tonight!" The one he was really dog-styling marveled as he shoved it all the way in to Miss Alvina with his eyes shut.

Morgana purred, "I'm beginning to believe you, now. No man could get that hard and move it so fine if he'd really been with that slant-eyed hussy working at the Golden Dragon!"

"I told you I hadn't been anywheres near that chop suey joint in recent memory and, for the record, the last time I ate there I was with another white lady, a reporter gal I never even kissed."

The one he was humping laughed like one of her meaner orphans and replied, "Who did you think spread those stories about you and that pretty Chinese waitress? I believe you never did this to that newspaper girl, now. You were right about hell having no fury. But, tell me, how come you managed not to add that poor thing to your score?"

He snorted and said, "Kids keep score. I only screw my friends and I could tell she was likely to brag about me when she intimated she'd once turned down a proposal of marriage from the late James Butler Hickok. She called him Wild Bill, like that pathetic Martha Jane Canary they buy drinks for as Calamity Jane. *She* claims Hickok proposed to *her*. I reckon neither knew him well enough to know he had a wife back east. But he did. Her name was Augusta Lake and she was a lady bareback rider he'd met touring in a vaudeville show with Bill Cody and other famous former buffalo hunters. Reckon they had to do *something* for a living, once

126

they'd thinned the herds down to where you really need to *hunt* for buffalo, these days."

She gasped threw gritted teeth, "Screw all the buffalo or, better yet, screw me, for I am almost there!"

That made two of them. So he rolled her on her bare back to finish up right with her shapely ankles crossed over the nape of his neck.

But, being a woman, once they were cuddled side by side, sharing an after-coming cheroot, she naturally asked if the horse thieves he was after might be out-of-work buffalo hunters, seeing so many wild men of the west had started out in that bloody trade.

He placed the cheroot to her lips as he thoughtfully mused, "Hard to say. Betwixt the wars betwixt the blue and gray or red and white, we've an oversupply of restless men, and women, trained in the use of firearms. When Uncle John Chisum warned the Apache to leave his trail hands alone, he bragged to them his Jingle Bob, alone, has more guns on its payroll than the U.S. Army has west of the Mississippi. Like I said, Uncle John was bragging. But not by much. There *are* more lean and hungry gunslicks than army troopers out this way. So how many mean civilians could be in the market for cavalry mounts?"

She passed the cheroot back to idly ask, "Doesn't the army buy horses like that, darling?"

He snorted, "Well, sure they do, but not government stock, already branded U.S. and . . . I'll be dunked in the Great Salt Lake if I don't think you just suggested the first answer that just might work!"

Chapter 15

Neither his gracious hostess nor his superior's wife would have been pleased if Longarm had shown up at Billy Vail's house at that hour, and, had the hour been more reasonable, he still had some loose ends to tie up before he stuck his neck out. So he disgraced his hostess some more and she seemed pleased as punch.

In the morning she served waffles with sorghum syrup and her own sweet self to him in bed before she had to catch another streetcar out to Arvada. She asked him to give her a head start and leave later, lest her neighbors talk. He knew more about neighbors than she did, but it was early, yet, so what the hell and he really enjoyed a long tub bath after all that time in the field.

He hadn't been asked to change back to his infernal tweed suit, yet. So he left Morgana's walk-up dressed more for the parts of town he was headed in his travel-dusty denim jeans and jacket. His .44-40 rode more openly on his left hip under the bolero-length denim jacket. So he got more thoughtful stares than usual as he made his way along the busy walks of a city waking up to go to work.

As he approached the nearby county morgue Longarm

saw a rubber-tired hearse out front, with its black team wearing feedbags as if they might be there a spell. Before he could pass on by, the young Widow Penn came out with a tall drink of water dressed to immitate Abe Lincoln on a gloomy occasion. When she spotted Longarm and yoo-hooed him, he cut back to tick his hat brim at her and declare he was at her service.

The pretty taffy blonde looked sort of green around the gills that morning. He understood why when she told him, "I've just come from cold storage after identifying my dead brother. They refused to release his body to Mister VanCouver, here, before someone from the family signed all sorts of papers stating it was really him! Have you ever heard of such nonsense?"

To which Longarm was forced to answer, "I have, ma'am. It happens a heap. It's all too easy to be mistaken about faces as are still alive, and folk are forever being found dead with identification papers that might or might not go with them."

She protested, "But Edward was in the custody of the law when he was killed! You were with him at the time!"

He nodded but said, "I reckon they feel it's better to be safe than sorry and I don't ride for Denver County, Miss Alvina."

He glanced at the undertaker to add, with a questioning eyebrow up, "Suffice it to be resolved that they're letting you have the remains, now?"

Undertaker VanCouver's stock went up a notch in Longarm's estimation when he quietly replied, "I mean to drive Miss Alvina back to the Vail home before we move Mister Lockwood. The county coroner, ah, ordered an autopsy."

Longarm grimaced and murmured, "I understand they get paid piecework rates. It's been nice talking with the both of you, but I have to get it on over to the railroad yards."

Alvina asked if he headed there in search of her brother's killers. When he allowed he might be she said she wanted to tag along with him. He said, "You go along with Mister VanCouver, here, and I'll be proud to fill you and Marshal Vail in as soon as I find anything out. I know you bust broncs and pack a Remington Repeater saddle gun, Miss Alvina, but I work best alone in parts where I already have my own hide to worry about."

So she said she'd hold him to that promise and he was free to forge on over to the Union Station.

It was called the *Union* Station because a whole bunch of different railroad lines converged there in a bodacious tangle of switch points and sidings to serve Denver in a manner that might have meant pcace to the world if different nations had been able to work together so sensible for mutual profit. Instead of forcing travelers to pass through customs inspections when they changed lines, the railroad dispatchers worked to transfer passengers and even rolling stock from one line to another in such a smooth manner that heaps of folk rode trains from New York City to Frisco without knowing they'd done so aboard four different railroad rights of way.

He didn't want to go to Frisco or New York City, so Longarm scouted up the yard boss who got to read all the dispatch orders as trains of all descriptions rolled in and out of Denver's sprawling yards.

He and Boss Emerson, in charge of that shift, went back a ways to begin with and Longarm offered the older man a cheroot before he got down to brass tacks, to show some respect before he made any demands.

Once they were lounging in the open doorway facing the yards, Longarm filled the railroader in on recent mass movements of military mounts.

Boss Emerson pondered some before he decided,

"Horses in modest amounts ride the rails in all directions, Deputy Long. But if the pure truth be known, and don't ever mention this to anybody writing for *Ned Buntline's Western Tales*, Denver ships more livestock east in the form of *sheep* than horses, or even cows. You can save money herding cows on up the Goodnight Trail to Wyoming, to load 'em direct aboard the U.P. at Cheyenne. But it would take forever for a sheep to walk that far and so—"

"I was asking about horses. Army bays standing better than fourteeen hands, but mayhaps mixed in with other horseflesh to blur the image?"

Boss Emerson said, "I'm sorry I already lit this tobacco, old son, for you ain't the first lawman to ask that same question and the answer would still be the same. They don't ship many horses of any description *east*. They're more inclined to ship Tennessee walkers, Thoroughbreds, and such *west*, from Kentucky, Missouri, or, of course, Tennessee. The stud spread out here can sell riding stock as fast as they can breed and bust 'em, out this way in a natural seller's market for most anything on four hooves!"

Longarm demured, "Not the sort of mounts run off from Camp Weld. We've asked. The late Hoss MacLeod never had more than a dozen such bays in his corral at one time, and they were noticed, surrounded by stickerbrush he'd planted deliberate. But let's go back over what you said before about mounts in more modest numbers riding every which way by rail. Are you talking about *individual* horses, riding *alone*?"

Boss Emerson nodded and replied, "How else would a mounted passenger get anywheres serious by rail? Unless he wants to abandon his pony, or sell it for a song at distressed prices, a trail herder headed back to say some Texas spread buys a combination ticket on a crosscountry train made up of passenger and freight cars.

Then he gets aboard a passenger coach with his baggage and they put his mount aboard one of the stock cars trailing downwind of the passengers and freight. Once his train arrives at his Texican stop, they both get off and he rides on home in the saddle, a whole lot sooner than he'd have ever made it home on horse back, see?"

Longarm said, "I thought that's what you meant. I've traveled that way myself, now and again. Now that I study on it, nobody asked me to prove ownership of my baggage, animate or inanimate. So how tough would it be for one lone horse thief to ride out of Denver, day or night, with just one stolen horse of any description?"

The yard boss shrugged and allowed it didn't sound that tough to him.

He observed, "Nobody working for any of the railroads out of here frets all that much about well-behaved paying passengers or baggage that ain't likely to explode or catch fire. No one railroader has much to do with both a traveling horseman and his horse, riding in separate cars aboard a combination train. There's usually more than one saddle bronc, at least a dozen dogs, and a shanghai rooster or more back in the stock car. The conductor might or might not connect a particular critter with a particular passenger as he's punching combination tickets. But don't hold me to that, and not even the Pinkerton dicks riding the lines pay much attention to anyone or anything that ain't making *trouble*."

Longarm nodded thoughtfully and decided, "Now I've got to work on all the extra help the gang would need. Riders taking the risks of a raid on a military reservation wouldn't be content with modest returns. But you find many a hobo willing to work cheap at easy chores around any railroad yards. Say you split up a stolen remuda amongst different hideouts and gave a bo a little drinking money and a ticket to other parts for him, his new work duds, and a mount he'd never have to ride, once they got off wherever the leader of the gang's been sending them?"

Boss Emerson soberly replied, "Wouldn't take much in the way of sweat brains on the bo's part. Wouldn't be any risk to the real crooks if their tool got caught aboard the combination with the stolen horse. As soon as they knew he'd been caught, nobody would be there to meet his train."

Longarm said, "Old Billy Vail is going to expect more of me than smart guessing. Is Denver P.D. still turning a blind eye on that hobo jungle west of the yards, just north of the approaches to the South Platte Bridge?"

Boss Emerson shrugged and said, "They're going to camp *somewheres* near the tracks and it's easier to keep an eye on 'em when they camp in a bunch where nobody else gives a shit. But do you really expect a hobo who's been stealing horses to talk to you about it?"

Longarm shrugged and said, "Not the ones who've snuck stolen horses out of town for the more serious horse thieves, even if any of 'em ever came back. But I've noticed, shooting pool or sipping cider in a house of ill repute, that for every knockaround drifter real crooks recruit, they have to talk to others, heaps of others, without the nerve to go along with anything more serious than begging or petty theft. They can hang you for horsetheft in Colorado. So there's just no saying how many hobos you'd have to ask to get one to aid and abet you."

They shook on that and parted friendly. Longarm knew better than to head for a hobo jungle empty-handed. He left the Union Station by way of its east entry facing Wynkoop Street and headed south along the same with a view to following 16th Street over to the South Platte Bridge approaches with some grub and whistle-wettings.

It wasn't as easy as that. He had the redbrick walls

133

of the railroad station to his right as far as the corner of Wynkoop and 16th. So he crossed over to hotels and shop fronts facing the station, peering at the plate glass ahead for any indications of a grocery or liquor store. He saw neither, but there seemed to be another cuss, dressed cow, right behind him, which seemed reasonable enough. But after that the stranger under the Texas-crowned ten-gallon Stetson had a Winchester yellowboy cradled over one elbow, which didn't. Longarm had been getting funny looks in downtown Denver because of the gun he was packing bold as brass. He was allowed to because he was the law. The stranger under the Tex-ican hat didn't seem to know, or didn't seem to care, that Denver P.D. frowned on toting guns around town and were inclined to ask you how come you were doing that.

But as he kept a wary eye on the sinister reflection of the man behind him, Longarm reflected that it was not a federal matter, as long as the son of a bitch kept the muzzle of that yellowboy pointed polite.

He worked his way to the corner, paying attention to each and every shop window he passed, to see that, sure enough, just a tad farther on past the cross-street, hung the sign advertising bottled goods, with a delicatessen just beyond. So he crossed the busy intersection through a gap in the moving traffic, noting in another shop window across the way that the mysterious stranger with the well-known brand of saddle gun had broken into a run as well, albeit catty-corner, to fetch up on the far side of 16th on the west side of Wynkoop.

Longarm didn't care, at first. It seemed easier to keep an eye on the cuss as they moved along opposite sides of the north-south street at about the same pace.

Then Longarm had made it to the liquor store and the stranger across the way suddenly seemed to need a new hat. He ducked into a millinery facing the liquor store from the far side. It was called a millinery instead of a hat shop because it sold fancy hats to ladies.

The burly Irish-looking gent running the liquor store asked Longarm what he could do for him. Longarm flashed his badge as he said he was in the market for a jug of rum, eventually, but needed to use their back entrance at the moment.

Before the burly Irishman could cloud up and rain all over him, the taller but leaner Longarm explained, "I'm after an outlaw gang. They've tried once or mayhaps twice before to gun me. I mean to ask a man with a gun in that millinery across the way what he had in mind for me as I came back out your front door with my purchase. I somehow sense that's what he's looking forward to, right now."

So the liquor store owner showed Longarm out the back way and from there it was duck soup simple to make his way along a back alley, across Wynkoop a block down, and then along another alley to the back of that millinery, which naturally had its own back entrance.

So as Longarm eased forward through the perfumed gloom meant for more delicate customers with his six-gun drawn, he came upon the tense scene presented by two middle-aged ladies cowering in a corner near a counter.

A figure outlined against the glass front door stood with his back to Longarm with that yellowboy at port arms as he waited for his target to emerge from the liquor store across the way.

Longarm had the drop on the cuss and wanted to take him alive. But one of the dear little ladies spotted him standing there with yet another gun and screamed, "Don't kill us! Please don't kill us!"

So the other man with a gun whirled around to shush

her, locked eyes with Longarm, and they both fired at the same time.

Both guns were chambered for the same popular .44-40 rounds. The one aimed at Longarm ticked the empty holster on his left hip to blow one serious hole in the plaster behind him.

Longarm's round took his would-be assassin over the heart to send him through the front door to land limp as a wet noodle amid shards of sharp shattered glass.

Longarm stepped through the busted-out doorway to regard what he'd just wrought morosely as a uniformed roundsman from Denver P.D. came running from the Union Station.

Longarm flashed his badge and said, "I'd be the law, too. I'm not at all sure who this cuss at our feet might be. I've been playing hide-and-seek with a whole bunch of horse thieves, see?"

The copper badge nodded soberly down at the dead man on the walk to quietly reply, "I do indeed and, offhand, I'd say you must be getting warm!"

Chapter 16

There were advantages and disadvantages to shooting it out within sight of the Union Station. It brought one hell of a crowd within minutes and said crowd soon included that pesky Reporter Crawford from the *Denver Post* and the burly Segeant Nolan from Denver P.D.

Nolan owed his stripes to listening to Longarm that time the two of them had worked on a broad day burglary. So, taking charge as the laconic Longarm reloaded in front of that millinery, Nolan grimaced at the tall Texican hat in the gutter to declare, "Sure, and I knew this Kerry man would come to a bad end. You know what they say about Kerry men. But I never expected him to die in such a distinguished fashion. I warned him more than once he'd be done in by another mad dog."

Longarm reholstered his six-gun as he asked, "What do they say about Kerry men and who did you say he was?"

Nolan replied, "Everyone knows County Kerry is famous for its fools and it must be something in the waters of Killarney. His name was Jack Sullivan and they called him Sulky Jack because of his sunny disposition. But, sure, why am I the one to be after telling you all this?

Was he fibbing when he claimed to be the fastest gun north of the Arkansas Divide?"

Reporter Crawford, even burlier, but dressed in loud checks instead of Uniform Blue, had been listening, pad and pencil in hand. So even as he wrote it down they heard him chortle, "Denver's own Longarm shoots it out with Sulky Jack Sullivan and guess who wins!"

The penny dropped in the back of Longarm's brain, inspiring him to mutter, "Aw, shit. I recall such bullshit making the rounds over to the Larimer Street Arcade. But this pistol punk was never wanted on any federal charges."

"Denver couldn't prove any of his brags, either." Nolan agreed with a thin smile, adding, "He'd have surely become a federal want had he been the winner, just now!"

Reporter Crawford, who spent more time listening to bullshit making the rounds, said, "That's for certain! Rumor had it Sulky Jack Sullivan had gunned two lawmen down in New Mexico Territory for fun and profit, back in '78. A sheriff Brady and a Deputy Hindman, I think they said, if I heard them right."

Longarm snorted, "You heard them wrong, or they had it wrong. The ones they indicted *in absentia* for the assassination of Sheriff William Brady of Lincoln County were Richard Brewer, the leader of the bunch, and his sidekick, Henry McCarty, also known as William Bonney."

Reporter Crawford gasped, "Aren't you talking about Billy The Kid?"

Longarm shrugged and said, "Some call him that. Dick Brewer was killed in a shoot-out with Buckshot Roberts before they could try him for the killing of Brady and Hindman. The kid is still at large, for now. This poor dead asshole oozing over the edge of the curb was never mixed up in that recent Lincoln County War.

I know this because we have wanted fliers on the few survivors, over to the federal building. New Mexico is still a territory, under federal jurisdiction."

Reporter Crawford insisted, "Whoever Sulky Jack was working for, I don't think they liked you, Deputy Long!"

Longarm agreed, "That seems plain enough. Don't you reckon we ought to get him off the street before he starts to spoil, Sergeant Nolan?"

Nolan said, "First someone from our new detective squad will want to be after having pictures taken and drawing chalk marks around the dumb dead Kerry man. Then it's off to the morgue with him, and to whom shall we be releasing the remains?"

Longarm said, "Ouch! Let's hope some kith and kin come forward, or mayhaps he's really wanted somewhere and the county's welcome to the bounty if they'd care to plant him in Potter's Field. Can't that wait until we know more about all this bullshit?"

Nolan cheerfully replied, "Sure and he's not going anywhere until we've had plenty of time to backtrack him to the wet rock he was crawling out from under this morning. Leave it to me, and, sure, why not be somewhere else so I can be doing the talking when the pencil pushers from the coroner's office get here?"

They shook on that and Longarm crossed back over to the liquor store to complete the errand Sulky Jack Sullivan had interrupted. He got that jug of rum and, deciding to skip the delicatessen, swung wide of the still crowded intersection of 16th and Wynkoop to follow 15th Street west to the banks of the South Platte, littered with all sorts of crap washed downstream by highwater, with crackwillow, ragweed, and cockleburr sprouting wherever they could strike root through all the driftwood and trash.

He made his way under the 16th Street Bridge, where

a pack of rats as big as cats paid him no heed as they dined on a drowned sheepdog the muddy river had brought downstream to them. Longarm preferred to live and let live, when you let him, so he resisted the temptation and passed by with his six-gun holstered and the peace offering of white rum cradled by his left forearm.

He found the hobo jungle he was looking for in a clump of brushy resprouted willows just north of the bridge, with the river directly to the west and the railroad yards a tad further off to the east across open acres of ballast and cinders the yard crews kept clear with periodic burns.

The bos had improvised canvas shelter-halves, lean-tos, and salvaged shipping crates among the willows. As Longarm approached he saw an even half dozen bos seated around a small smokeless fire, watching a tin can atop the coals as it bubbled and squeaked. Few real life hobos looked at all like that caricature striding along under a plug hat with a bandana-wrapped bundle on a stick over his shoulder. Real hobos didn't like to duck shotgun pellets of local lawmen that much. So they tried to resemble working men, mayhaps down on their luck for the moment but looking for work, not somebody's chickens, and in point of fact, most bos *would* work just long enough in one place to be on their way with a full belly and a little pocket jingle, provided you didn't ask them to work too hard.

The bunch Longarm found by the river that morning all bore some faint resemblance to field workers or cow hands, assuming either had hocked anything fine as a tooled leather belt or a half-decent hat. Not one of them looked up at him as he joined them around the fire. He knew they were waiting for him to declare his road moniker. So he announced in a friendly enough tone, "I'd be U.S. Deputy Marshal Custis Long and I'm not here to give any of you gents a hard time."

140

One of the older bos rose from the fire, not looking at Longarm as he turned away, muttering, "I got nothing to say to no federal bulls!"

To which Longarm pleasantly replied, "Why don't you just go fuck your hand whilst the rest of us split this jug of rum, then?"

It worked. The old bo turned back with a hopeful look and some of the others were smiling up at Longarm, now. So he hunkered down by the fire and when their obvious spokesman returned from his flounce-off to squat beside him, Longarm handed over the jug, suggesting his elder host might prefer to do the honors.

Then Longarm kept his mouth shut and his ears open as the jug was passed around more than once. Whenever it came his turn, Longarm put spit-slicked earthenware near his lips but passed the jug on untasted. Aside from not wanting to catch anything awful, Longarm knew there was only a gallon of hundred proof to be shared, coming to a little over a pint a hobo, and hobos tended to drink more than, say, Sunday school teachers. But a quart of a hundred-proof would have killed that poor Sunday school teacher, and the passed-around jug had his half dozen hobos drunk enough to sing Christmas carols in no time.

Longarm didn't want them to sing about sleigh rides in the summertime. So after one of the younger bos fell over backwards to start snoring up through the willow branches, Longarm felt it was time to bring up the topic of crimes and misdemeaners. There seemed to be no objections. For as that older one they naturally called Pop had decided, their new pal might be a fucking bull but he was all heart.

After that the only matter before the house was pinning one fact firmly down. As Longarm had hoped, the bunch of them had heard talk about easy money, riding a pony from Hoss MacLeod's stud farm into town, or

141

meeting another bo who had, having paid a passenger-livestock fare ahead of time so's you and the pony could get right aboard. But after that none of them knew where MacLeod had been paying his casual workers to get off with those obviously stolen mounts. None of the bos he'd caught up with had hired on with MacLeod because they'd heard a bo could hang for shady horsemanship in Colorado, and hence they hadn't heard any further details from the late Hoss MacLeod.

He asked in a desperately casual voice whether any of them had ever been approached to perform similar chores for another horse trader of MacLeod's ilk.

Old Pop confided with a toothless grin, "Hoss MacLeod was all there was if you wanted to buy or sell hot horseflesh in these parts. I once heard tell of a breed gal trying to horn in on his game. But Hoss bought her off, scared her off, or maybe shot her off. Hoss wasn't one for the sharing of trade secrets. The bulls killed old Hoss the other night, I heard, so what does it matter what he did to that breed gal?"

"It don't matter to this child!" Longarm lied, adding, "I suspect I know who we're talking about. What did you say they called her?"

"Comanche Rose," said the old bleary-eyed bo, adding wistfully, "Pretty little thing as long as you like dark meat, and they did say that whilst Comanche Rose only fucked her friends, she didn't have an enemy in this world."

"But you said Hoss MacLeod ran her off, or worse," Longarm objected.

The older man helped himself to another heroic swig of hundred proof, muttered, "Shit, I don't know what Hoss MacLeod did about that breed gal and what difference does it make? He's dead and she's long gone and I don't give a shit. I ain't got any hot horseflesh for sale and I sure ain't fixing to buy none!"

Then Longarm found himself talking to himself. The two survivors on the far side of the fire were staring through him, not at him, as he got to his feet to say, not unkindly, "*Hasta la vista*, motherfuckers." Then he turned to walk directly across the railroad yards, through the Union Station and up 17th Street, all the way to the Statehouse grounds, seven furlongs off, and hence along the crest of Capitol Hill to Billy Vail's private residence, where, as he'd hoped, he found the young Widow Penn with the older Mrs. Vail, who was expecting her man home for his noon dinner directly.

As they waited on the front porch, sipping lemonade and Scotch shortbread in moderation, since together they were too sweet by half, Longarm told the two women a little of what he'd found out so far.

They agreed it appeared the late Hoss MacLeod had been the local king of horse thieves until newcomers led or fronted by the mysterious Comanche Rose had tried to horn in on him. Longarm suspected, and they allowed it made sense, that the bunch Comanche Rose was riding with had appeared on the scene with stolen horses for sale, felt the crooked Hoss MacLeod was making the easy money at less risk, and felt they'd do a better job at stealing and dealing with fewer middle men.

Alvina stared thoughtfully down at her lemonade as she decided, "That strawberry blonde lured the greedy Hoss MacLeod into the trap set by her taffy blonde confederate with your help. So that makes at least three wild women working . . . together or led by this mysterious Indian woman?"

Longarm replied, "More likely a breed, if not Mexican or colored, Miss Alvina. Folk don't talk down to Comanche if they know a thing about Comanche and it's a caution how many Mexican or colored folk would as soon be called a Redskin as a greaser or a nigger. So I'll tell you what I think Comanche Rose might be as

143

soon as I catch up with her, if she's still alive."

Alvina pointed out, bless her smart little ass, "Hoss MacLeod would have never agreed to bid on those mounts from Camp Weld if he'd thought he was at feud with the gang. Isn't it more likely he just refused to cut them in and they pretended more respect than they really had for the greedy old Scotchman?"

Mrs. Vail quietly but firmly declared, "I'll thank you to bite your tongue, Widow Penn. It so happens my husband, Marshal William Vail, is of Scots descent, and his people were Highland, too, thank you very much!"

Longarm soothed, "Miss Alvina called MacLeod a *greedy* Scotchman, ma'am, and didn't Billy tell me, one time, that the Vails came out for Bonnie Prince Charlie whilst others, like the Clan MacLeod, held back?"

Mollified, Mrs. Vail asked if they'd like some more Scotch shortcake. They both refused. Their shortcake wasn't bad if you liked biscuits, as it tasted like butterscotch taffy. But he knew she catered to old Billy's old country tastes and some Scotch notions took a little getting used to. Old Billy drank whiskey that smelled like smoke and smoked cigars that smelled like tarred rope in spite of his sweet tooth when it came to pastries.

As if the tense discussion of his ancestry had been his stage cue, old Billy Vail in the flesh came stumping along the sandstone walk in his Justin boots and snuff-colored business suit, looking more like a banker fixing to do some serious riding than a Highland laddy. His sept of their clan had suffered some sea changes along the way from the mists of Alban to the sun-baked high plains of the American West. But he sure was puffing that evil black cigar as he spied them waiting out front for him and strode a mite faster.

As he mounted the steps he told Longarm, "I swear if you were entered in a horse race and somebody shot your horse out from under you, I'd still bet on you to place or show!"

"What did he do now, William?" asked Mrs. Vail in an amused tone.

The marshal said, "Shot a scamp with a hundred-dollar bounty on his head. The late Sulky Jack Sullivan killed a soiled dove in Dodge and her . . . protector posted the reward for his death, period. Said he'd never be satisfied with anything less than death by hanging or whilst resisting arrest. So Denver P.D. just agreed they'd be proud to say their Sergeant Nolan had been trying to arrest him, assisted by one Deputy Long, when the ornery cuss had simply refused to come along like a sensible gent. They figure they can plant him in Potter's Field for less than thirty dollars and drink to his memory with the change. But now we have to figure out why he was sent to kill this other rascal, and what they're worried about him knowing that the rest of us don't know, for Pete's sake!"

Longarm said, "We were just talking about that as we were waiting on you, Boss. I think I've got that part figured out. I wish the rest of it came so easy."

Chapter 17

The lady of the house suggested they all go inside for dinner. But her husband declared, "I can eat any time. Custis, here, says he has the answer to what's been eating me persistent!"

He propped a boot on the porch as he remained on the steps, ordering Longarm not to act so coy.

Longarm said, "Hoss MacLeod knew what Kansas Red looked like. He'd made a deal with her to bid on those military mounts from Camp Weld. But he's dead and nobody else we can hope to hear the truth from has claimed to see her close up. We've no idea what this Cherokee Rose may look like. But that third shemale member of the gang, pretending to be Miss Alvina, here, dealt with me, intimate, in broad day!"

"Custis Long, you ought to be ashamed!" gasped Billy's old woman.

Longarm soothed, "I ain't. She should have been. I saw her stark, all over, when she tried to compromise a federal official. So that makes me the one and only rider on our side who could identify at least one of the gang for certain, at some distance, see?"

Vail started to say something silly, then he nodded

soberly and conceded, "You're right. The rest of us took your word about the sister of Edward Lockwood being approached by other horse thieves and . . . Sorry, Miss Alvina."

The real Alvina nodded graciously and demurely replied, "Edward was a horse thief, I fear, albeit not a very smart one, and so now I'm having him shipped home to Ohio to await the Last Judgment with the rest of our family. I don't think he knew any of those wicked women. So why do you think they wanted to murder him?"

Longarm modestly suggested, "They might have been aiming for me, or he might have known that sweet, young thing under some other name. I doubt she'd have told him she was his sister. But she must have talked to someone who knew you both right well, Miss Alvina. The two of you didn't look at all alike, up close, but she had your family and more recent history down pat."

He glanced at Vail to add, "She tried to compromise any possible arresting officer. So she had to let me have a real good look at her. But whether Hoss MacLeod or Miss Alvina's brother ever laid eyes on that particular member of the gang, I'm the only one who'd recognize her in a crowd right now."

"I can see why they're out to stop your clock." Vail growled, "Get to what else they might be up to!"

Longarm sighed and said, "That ain't as obvious, but a picture does seem to be slowly emerging from the mists. The late Hoss MacLeod was a receiver of stolen goods. He let others take the risks of stealing. So they'd been selling hot horseflesh to him, dealing through that other gal they call Kansas Red, to hear him tell as he lay dying."

"But how come he was buying so many military mounts off 'em?" asked Vail, shaking his head as he added, "I'd say a big army bay, broke to gunfire instead of trail herding, would be nigh impossible to sell at any real profit."

Longarm said, "I noticed. MacLeod could have only been selling unusual horseflesh in wholesale lots to an unusual buyer. I can't see *our* remount service buying stock stolen from U.S. military reservations, and, for all their faults, the Canadian Mounties wouldn't deal with a Colorado crook. So who's left?"

Vail brightened but snapped, "What are you waiting for, a kiss good-bye? I can tell you from my ranger days that the nearest Mex Remount station would be just outside El Paso. The El Paso south of the Rio Grande, not the one on this side. Wire when you get to the border and by then I'll have had Henry type up your travel orders. Remember, if anyone ever asks, that you lost the onionskins Henry gave you before he filed your field mission, official."

Longarm rose, ticked his hat brim to both the ladies, and tripped past Vail down the steps. He turned to his right as soon as he got on back to the north-south walk along Sherman, meaning to head for his own digs by way of the Cherry Creek bridge at 14th and Larimer. Before he got to the next corner he heard boot heels suddenly overtaking him on the sandstone slabs and paused to turn and tick his hat brim some more as Alvina Penn nee Lockwood caught up with him, flushed and panting some.

She gasped, "Where are you going? What's going on? What was all that about the Mexican Remount Service?"

He politely replied, "I got to keep going, Miss Alvina. Marshal Vail will be proud to explain it all to you back at the house."

She snapped, "Pooh, I guess I can walk as fast as you if I have to. Tell me along the way. Where are we going?"

Longarm chuckled and they started to stride on as he

told her, "*I* got to head down Mexico way. I'm headed for my furnished digs to pack. After that I have a night combination to catch, discreet, in case they have yet another gunslick covering the regular boarding platforms at the Union Station. They have the edge that I only know one member of their bunch on sight. *You* got to steer well clear of me. If I have to spell it out any clearer than that you sure must be stupid, no offense!"

She dimpled up at him to say, "None taken. I've done all I can here in Denver for my poor black-sheep kid brother. Some distant kin will be meeting his casket when it gets off in Ohio. So can't I ride at least as far as Colorado Springs with you?"

He insisted, "You can't even come upstairs with me at my rooming house. My picky old landlady has a suspicious mind."

He felt no call to concede any just cause to the dear old soul. But fair was fair and he had shot that outlaw in her shithouse and busted through her bedsprings with that frisky Mex gal. So he sincerely meant it when he told a might pretty little thing she wouldn't be welcome at his rooming house at the moment.

Alvina proved herself well legged-up when Longarm turned left near the statehouse grounds to roll downhill on his own long legs. She had to take more steps to keep up. But she managed, gasping, "I can wait outside whilst you pack! Why are we suddenly so certain Hoss MacLeod was selling horses to the Mexican Army and, even if he was, how come the horse thief he was buying army horses off of wanted to put him out of business?"

Longarm told her, "To take over his business. He made the mistake of telling them, or he let them find out, about his steady, ready market for well-bred and battle-trained cavalry mounts. They might have figured it out for themselves and the dark gal they call Comanche Rose might well be a Mexican gal well-versed in

149

shady dealings along the border. For all the bad things they say about us, *Los Federales*, as you call the Mexican Regular Army, just loves to imitate the U.S. Cav. They're issued the same Schofield .45 horse pistols and the long-range Springfield .45-70 that can down an Apache, or a discontented Mexican citizen, at a mile."

He slowed down a tad as he saw how tough it was to gallop and talk at the same time. That allowed her to gasp, "I want you to arrest the ones who murdered my brother, here in Denver, not their confederates down by the border, durn it!"

Longarm soothed, "Same bunch. Why would they want to hang around these parts after putting the biggest crooked dealer in these parts out of business? Don't you see they wanted to make it impossible for the Mex Remount Service to buy stock from their local source of supply? I've no doubt they've been buying good cavalry stock anywhere they can. Crooked remount officers MacLeod was dealing with never came all the way north to Colorado for the stolen stock. MacLeod was sneaking it down to wherever it's been crossing the border. The gang, let's call it Kansas Red's gang for lack of a better handle, couldn't use the late Hoss MacLeod's local spread and stockyard contacts if it wanted to. They gave the whole show away when they sent your double to me to double-cross him. Having done so, they'd have no further need to operate this far north. With both the U.S. and Mexican Cavs out in force along the border this summer on account of Victorio and his Bronco Apache, there must be dozens of army outposts to raid, way closer to their ready market for cavalry mounts!"

She marveled, "Ooh, you're so sneaky-minded! Now all we have to do is warn all the army posts to the south to be on guard against horse thieves, right?"

He wearily replied, "They're already on guard. Every military post on either side of the Mississippi issues a

150

sentry with a Springfield the same general orders every guard mount."

As they were crossing Broadway at the foot of the slope, Longarm thought back to earlier times when he'd thought the world was run on the level and softly intoned, "General Order Number One: I shall walk my post in a military manner, keeping always on the alert and reporting all that happens on or near my post to the Corporal of the Guard!"

She didn't recall any teenaged military duties. She said she was puzzled about that gang being led by women. Another blonde, a redhead, and a swarthy brunette, so far.

Longarm said, "Queen Victoria gets to lead that bodacious British Empire and she don't look so tough. But we don't know for certain that any of those gals associated with the bunch are anything but scouts or contacts. Kansas Red, Comanche Rose, and your mysterious other self may be no more than doxies of the sneakier ringleaders. As you can see, we don't have one proper name for any member of a gang of uncertain size and composition. But farther along, as the old church song says, we may know more about it. I know it sounds tedious, and sometimes it is, but you can only eat any apple one bite at a time."

They naturally went over the same bare-bones more than once by the time they got to his frame rooming house on the unfashionable side of Cherry Creek. She was trying to be a sport. But he could tell the rich young widow didn't think much of the neighborhood.

That gave him a grand notion. When they got as far as the front hallway, Longarm pointed up the sort of gloomy stairwell to decide, "You might as well come on up to my room, seeing it's so dusty down here and my landlady ain't around."

He expected her to come up with a gracious excuse.

But she just headed up the stairs ahead of him. So he followed with mixed feelings. He wanted to get rid of her and when a lady wouldn't take polite discouragement for an answer there were other ways to shoo a pussy.

She tried to hide it, but he caught the slight wrinkle of her pretty lip as she compared his inexpensive furnished digs to her town house in Manitou Springs or even her main house on the S Bar P. He waved at the bedstead taking up most of the space in the one room and told her to take a load off her pretty little derriere whilst he checked the contents of his saddlebags. He explained, "I still have my McClellan checked in the baggage room at the Union Station, but as I told you when we got in from Colorado Springs, it's dumb to leave saddlebags or a good saddle gun where weak-natured souls might be tempted."

She nodded but asked, "How did you know you'd be going back out in the field so soon?"

He draped the saddlebags over the footrails of the bed and drew his Winchester '73 from its boot as he shrugged and replied, "I never expected any of the bunch to lurk around Denver, once they'd used me to rid them of the competition. That blonde pretending to be you might be lurking somewhere closer, as somebody more socially acceptable. That would account for their most recent attempt on my life here in Denver."

He saw he'd assumed rightly that nobody had fired his saddle gun whilst he was out and slid it back in its boot, continuing. "It's just as likely they wanted to gun a lawman here in Denver to convince the law they're all still in town. I got to change my underwear, now. You're welcome to stay and watch if you insist on tagging along with me to El Paso. I hope you understand there's no way any couple of any gender can avoid getting sort of . . . intimate, once they're sneaking up on others together?"

She nodded soberly and said, "You're speaking to a woman who's lived with a natural man and I like to rinse my own unmentionables out when I can."

Things weren't working out exactly as planned. Longarm chuckled fondly, pointed at the washstand in a far corner, and suggested, "Be my guest, if that long walk's made you sweaty down yonder."

So as he removed his gun rig and commenced to unbutton his shirt, the taffy blonde seated on his bedcovers calmly hoisted her skirts up around her shapely young hips to reveal lithe horsewoman's legs jay naked from boot tops to frilly cotton drawers, before she shifted her weight to slide her bare behind out of the same.

Longarm made no attempt to avert his eyes. He was trying to scare her off. So he was staring right down at the view when she slid her drawers down her lithe limbs to raise each boot out of them in turn, allowing him to determine that she, too, was blonde all over. Then she rose to let her skirts drop chastely back in place as she stepped over to the washstand to drop her frilly drawers in the bowl and poured water from the handy pitcher over them whilst Longarm went on shucking his own duds.

So when she turned around to face him, he was standing there in his birthday suit with his old organ grinder commencing to rise to the occasion, whether he commanded it to or not.

He tried not to grin like a mean little kid when she blanched at the sight and took a step backwards. He was sure she'd bolt for the door any second. But she gulped and managed, "Good heavens, there's certainly more to you than meets the eye!"

Then she reached down to get a good grip on her skirts and peel her summer frock off over her head, spilling a taffy blonde cascade in the process, as she demurely added, "Take it easy until I get used to it, won't you? It's been a while, and while it's wrong to speak ill of the dead, I fear my poor husband wasn't half the man you've turned out to be and, oh, my Lord, it's getting bigger!"

So he tried to be gentle as he took her in his bare arms to lower her back to the bedding as she weakly murmured, with her lips against his, "Wait! Maybe I would be safer here in Denver whilst you went on alone. I want justice for my poor murdered brother and I admit I might have been out for a little adventure for adventure's sake, but honestly. Custis, I don't think you'll ever get that thing inside me!"

And then he had, even as he cussed his own weak nature when his raging erection refused to let him take her up on her kind offer. For she was young and pretty, too, and had what they called a ring-dang-doo, as the old song went about another young buck who'd met a gal in another big old wild and wicked city that time.

The young widow's late cattle baron must have taught her the same old trail song, for she suddenly had her booted feet flung wide as she could get them as she seemed to be trying to buck him out of her love saddle, loudly sobbing, "You naughty girl, her mother said, you've gone and lost your maidenhead! There's only one thing left to do! Go advertise your ring-dang-doo!"

Chapter 18

So the fat was in the fire. But even though they'd been indiscreet, they still had to be discreet. When they met his landlady at the foot of the stairs, leaning thoughtfully on the handle of her dust mop, he introduced the gal she'd heard moaning and groaning upstairs as a material witness to a federal offense. The older woman sniffed and allowed she felt sure the young lady had witnessed something offensive.

Longarm was wearing clean underwear and fresh-if-faded trail denim to go with the saddlebags over one elbow and the Winchester he toted in his free hand. But most of Alvina's possibles were in her bags up at the Vail house and she hadn't put those wet frilly drawers back on as yet. So they stopped at more than one shop along the way to outfit her right in her own blue denim bolero and split skirts with a Spanish-crowned and railroad-brimmed Stetson a darker shade of tan than her hair, and, since she kept asking, a nickel-plated Schofield chambered for the Army .45-28 Shorts a green recruit or a determined young lady would be able to hold on to when it fired its fair-sized ball fairly gentle.

They'd spent some time getting to know one another,

in the biblical sense, at his rooming house. So it was mid afternoon by the time they'd worked their way aboard the south-bound combination Longarm had been keeping in mind all the while.

They never went through the redbrick Union Station. Longarm led her north to 19th Street, not as busy as 20th Street leading across the railroad yards to yet another river crossing, and strolled her south betwixt empty freight cars parked on sidings to where they could get on up to a signal tower shed where another pal worked.

After introducing Alvina and explaining their needs, Longarm told the railroader, "I'm hoping that if anyone's watching for us to board that Four-Forty-Five southbound combination they'll be expecting us to board her further south and hole up in a private compartment aboard one of your Pullman cars. So how do we sneak aboard the forward mail car to ride south with them other federal employees who'll be proud to have us, if they know what's good for 'em?"

The railroader had one of those new-fangled Bell telephones, since nobody could accuse the Denver & Rio Grande of being behind the times. So he had them fixed up within the hour. A puffer-billy switch engine ran an empty boxcar under the tower to carry them, concealed, down alongside the combination they were making up for the four-forty-five run. The postal service crew was expecting them with open arms, and a sliding door opened on the sunny side of their car. As they were helped aboard, Longarm was told that beat-up old army saddle in a far corner was his own, delivered by a colored redcap from the baggage room in the nearby station.

So Longarm handed out smokes to everyone but Alvina, having thought to stock up at a tobacco shop along the way, and then, just as he'd warned the pretty little gal, things got tedious as hell for a spell.

The four postal workers had chores to get back to. They kept from going crazy as sheepherders, cooped up for hours in a rolling mail car, by sorting the mail they were carrying. Mail got a rough cut at their main post office as it came in. The clerks there just noted the state an envelope was addressed to and, if it wasn't worth sorting some more in Denver, it got tossed in a sack bound for wherever. After the sacks were aboard a mail car headed for that state, the mail clerks riding with it dealt another hand to determine which post office along the line it was meant for. They dropped it in turn in the separate sacks they meant to drop off along the way. It kept everybody busy and worked smoother than it explained.

Having no mail to sort and no place she could sing trail songs about ring-dang-doos at the moment, Alvina found a pensive perch by one of the smaller grilled windows of the mail car. When she asked how come it was barred like a birdcage Longarm tersely explained how pests such as the Reno Brothers or, more recently, the Younger Brothers, Frank and Jesse James, were inclined to interfere with the U.S. Mails. He pointed at the stout Mosler safe under the sorting counter to add, "Road agents ain't out to read other people's mail, as a rule. But folk will send money orders and even cash by way of the U.S. Mails."

He knew she wasn't all that interested. But he didn't want the mail car crew to suspect they'd been fornicating long enough to suggest one another be still.

The car jolted into motion under them and Alvina said, "Oh, at last we're on our way!"

Longarm didn't bother to answer. She found out soon enough they'd only sidled over to the main boarding platform to take on passengers, now that the freight cars had been loaded.

Longarm didn't care. He'd known how tedious the trip south would be. They'd have to transfer and dogleg some to El Paso, thanks to the former rebel state of Texas having some catching up to do with its post-war railroad facilities. But Alvina broke the tedium by exclaiming from her perch by the window, "Good heavens! That looks like my Quirt McQueen getting on this very train with some Mexican girl and he ought to be ashamed of himself!"

Longarm moved over, sudden, but as he joined her at the grilled window, the couple she'd remarked upon had already boarded, and were out of their line of sight.

Longarm said, "I give up. Who's Quirt McQueen and how come he ought to be ashamed of himself?"

She explained, "He's one of my wranglers at the S Bar P. I allow him and my other married riders separate quarters and, last count, Quirt and his squaw had four papooses crawling the floor."

"He's married up with an Indian?" Longarm asked, adding, "Might she be Ute and, either way, are you sure that wasn't her or some in-law with him, just now?"

Alvina said, "I hope she turns out to be an in-law if she's another Indian. She looked more Mex. Quirt's wife is an Arapaho breed, and so is he, now that you mention it. What difference might her tribe make?"

Longarm explained, "Ute and Comanche speak the same lingo. Arapaho and Cheyenne speak western dialects of Algonquin. That don't mean the sultry brunette you just spotted with a man who handles horses for a living couldn't get called Comanche Rose, if she asked polite."

The lady the suspect wrangled for gasped, "Good heavens! Are you suggesting one of my own riders could be mixed up with those horse thieves?"

To which he could only reply, "Your kid brother was, and you and your segundo, Sandy Bowmore, agree your brother spent some time at your S Bar P trying to make do as a wrangler. But like that church song says, farther along, we'll know more about it. We're only a few stops from Colorado Springs, where they'll be getting off if they were only up this way for a visit. If they don't get off, I'll wait till we stop for water this side of Pueblo and have me a look at the stock car way in back of us."

She asked why he didn't run back right away, before the train left the Denver yards.

He sighed and said, "If you aim to go very far with me you're going to have to start thinking like I do about such matters."

She smiled like Miss Mona Lisa and said she'd already gone as far as she dared with him and thought exactly the same way he did about that.

He chuckled fondly and explained, "They gave this war one time and I was invited to come. As you can plainly see, I lived through it. But it wasn't easy. There was lots to learn. And one of the first things I learned was not to run anywhere I could reach as easy with a bullet and not to run anywheres at all before I was certain I had to. You just heard me say they'd either get off or stay aboard at Colorado Springs. If they get off, with or without any ponies, I'll have no call at all to go back to the stock car. If they get off at Colorado Springs, it will be closer to sundown when I get off at that water stop and stroll back along the darker side of this train in the tricky gloaming light. If I meet up with an army bay back yonder I'll have plenty of time to wire ahead during the longer stop at Pueblo and the Provost Marshal's Office can have the train met by Military Police, with neither one of us having to show our hands so early in the game, see?"

She said she saw indeed, and, lowering her voice as

their train commenced to slowly click and clack away from the station, asked him, "How could any natural chessmaster like you throw all caution to the winds in bed like that?"

He calmly replied, "Hold the thought and later on I might be able to show you as good a time. But I ain't really all that reckless with the tender feelings of a pal, if you'll recall how I kept at least half my weight on my knees and elbows, most of the time."

She warned him not to tease her like that unless he had a much more private train ride in mind. He had to admit that, alas, they seemed stuck with things the way they were, for the time being. So they talked about the mystery mission of Quirt McQueen until they got into Colorado Springs and the son of a bitch got off there with a short plump pretty *escua*, as close as Longarm could come to the Plains Arapaho for Squaw. Peeking out at them, Longarm could see the tall hatchet-faced rider with the gal looked sort of Indian as well. Then a taller but even fatter *escua* spoiled it all by coming across the platform to meet them with open arms. Longarm guessed before Alvina told him that she had to be Quirt McQueen's wedded wife. So there went even a cow country scandal!

The combination started up again to roll on, slow, then on some more as Alvina, bless her restless bottom, fretted about how much more fun it would have been to hire a private compartment. She bitched that she had her infernal checkbook with her and that should push come to shove she could ask for a line of credit at any bank west of the Kansas line.

Longarm repeated his sage observations regarding the calm and orderly progress of an army on the march or a lawman in the field. When he said you had to get there first with the most pep and energy, she pouted that almost all the men she'd ever hired were just as slow and

160

pokey. So it was just as well he'd already poked her. For was commencing to nag, as some women were wont to, before he'd even poked her twice!

He never told any ladies that was one of the things about his love life that kept him single. They liked it better when he told them how reluctant he was to leave a pretty young widow behind and felt it best to wait until he retired from his gun-toting chores in the sweet by and by. That was partly true. He had been to a sobering number of funerals when you considered how much they paid any lawman. But he often worried how he'd ever find any woman fashioned from mortal clay who could just take a man the way they found him and let him go on being his own fool self.

By the time they got to that prairie water stop in the middle of nowheres he'd gotten so tired of her fidgets that he got off and walked back along the shady side to satisfy her soul and rest his ears. Hugging the sides of the Pullman cars and keeping his hat brim low, he felt sure nobody on board spotted him in the gathering dusk as he made it there and back.

Climbing back aboard the mail car as the freshly watered locomotive moved on with a mighty clanging, Longarm was wearing a might bemused expression as he rejoined the restless gal by her window perch.

When she asked him why he was looking at her so funny, he confessed, "Pure admiration, ma'am. It's a caution how easy it is for a man to get sot in his ways, thinking he knows it all until some bright kid asks him a question he only thought he had an answer for!"

She demanded he get to the point.

He said, "I just met up with a bay gelding, fifteeen hands at the withers, branded 808 and shod with army issue steel!"

She gasped, "Oh, Dear Lord! Quirt McQueen *was* up to something sneaky up in Denver!"

161

He soberly replied, "He was likely fetching some in-law gal home to his own kith and kin. By now they'll have boarded that narrow guage west. Horses ain't allowed to ride alone as baggage, Miss Alvina. Had McQueen got on with that army bay the horse would have been asked to get off with him at the Springs."

She whispered, "You weren't calling me Miss Alvina in your bed, you brute. Are you intimating there's another passenger back there on the way south with that cavalry mount?"

He nodded and said, "Ain't intimating it. Saying it. You can't send anything as freight in a baggage car. So we spoke too soon about that gang moving on from Denver lock, stock, and barrel. Billy Vail and me made the common lawman's mistake of trying to think like an average crook when we were both stuck with average intelligence. Having put Hoss MacLeod out of business the greedy rascals are out to liquidate his Denver inventory. They knew better than to go anywhere near Hoss MacLeod's stud farm. But, like him, they'd probably hid out scores of stolen cavalry mounts in separate warehouses, carriage houses, and so on. I can't say how many more they mean to sneak down Mexico way, but they're surely running another one down, aboard this very train!"

She asked what he meant to do about it.

He said, "Ain't certain. The passenger riding the other half of their split ticket could be another hobo or some out-of-work cow poke. I'm more interested in where they'll get off and who'll be waiting for them when and where they do. I can't do nothing before this train gets to Pueblo. When it does, I want you to get off and head back up the line for home. You never know how these things are likely to turn out, but they could be coming to a head sooner than we expected!"

162

She protested loud enough for one of the mail clerks to glance up from his sorting chores, "You can't put me off in Pueblo after dark! What will become of me? What will I do?"

He suggested, "I'd start with a bowl of chili across from the depot whilst I waited on the next northbound. You'll be reading in the papers whether I won or lost. But if I win I'll stop by on my way back to the office and tell you all about it, hear?"

She fussed about it the full hour it took them to hiss to a stop in Pueblo, where they'd be busting up the combination to route different cars different ways, as profit moved them. So he kissed her fondly but never left the tracks with her, lest he and that army bay wind up aboard different trains in the tricky light, as the sun went all the way down behind the black peaks to the west.

Longarm caught up with the conductor he wanted in the confusion of coupling and uncoupling under a blood-red sky. As soon as he discovered he had to move his gear to another mail car if he wanted to ride down to Texas with that stolen bay, he muttered, "Shit, there goes my chance to wire ahead that it ain't El Paso after all. What can you tell me about the gent who's claiming that big bay as his cowpony?"

The conductor said, "To begin with it ain't a gent, it's a lady, with a sidesaddle checked through with her bridle and saratoga. After that she said it was her show horse, not a cowpony. A gift, she allowed, from an admirer."

"I've reason to suspect I once admired her more," Longarm said with a thin smile. He asked if the lady in question might be blonde and had a seat number. The conductor allowed he had the hair right, but the lady had no seat number. She'd booked a private compartment to travel sort of exclusive. So Longarm allowed he could see why she might want to.

Then he headed back to gather up his gear, grinning wolfishly as he added to himself, "Now we know why you made them so proddy anywheres in the neighborhood of the Union Station!"

Chapter 19

Longarm had known where the train he'd boarded in Denver was bound for. So the mail car he had to get off was still bound for El Paso and the one tagging along with that army bay and Alvina's sneaky double was headed for the border crossing at Ojinaga, way down-stream from El Paso and better than two hundred miles east by crow.

Looking on the bright side as he settled in with the new postal crew aboard the other car, that mystery gal and that stolen cavalry mount would be getting off and hopefully be met by friends at Ojinaga on a sunny West Texas afternoon at the rate they were going. So Longarm borrowed some space at a sorting table to compose long and thoughtful telegrams to his home office, the army provost marshal at Fort Stockton, and, not certain he could count on federal help in such a dinky border town on such short notice, the Texas Rangers at Del Rio.

When the reformed combination stopped for water at the head of the Pecos Valley, Longarm wrapped his messages around a bunch of cheroots and asked the straw-boss of the water tower crew to send the wires for him, charged to his Denver office.

Then there was nothing to do but hunker down in a corner with his old saddle and somehow survive the next million years of tedium. He could only hope that taffy blonde with the vanilla ice-cream hide and chocolate eyes was as bored and fidgetsome back in that private compartment. He considered how private those Pullman compartments really were, and tried not to picture a gal he'd seen so much of parting that natural blonde thatch betwixt her legs with dainty fingers or something wilder. It hardly seemed fair, but due to their natural love juices, women got to pleasure themselves in way more artificial ways than menfolk. He had to chuckle fondly when he recalled that lonely homestead gal who'd told him he was built way better than her rolling-pin handles and much more romantic than your average ear of corn. But a grown man would feel silly pleasuring himself in a rolling mail car under a swinging oil lamp. So he told himself not to think about that taffy blonde back yonder, or the other blonde he'd parted with in Pueblo.

He finally dozed off, only to wake up cold and stiff as they stopped somewhere in the night, repeated the process a dozen more times, and then it was daybreak, and at least he got to perch on a stool by another grilled window and admire the scenery until it commenced to repeat its fool self. Stirrup-high chaparral punctuated by yucca stalks and mesquite-lined dry-washes did get tedious in time. So Longarm and the mail crew consumed more bottled beer and stale sandwiches along the way than they really needed to, since dickering for the same at the longer stops was a way to kill whole minutes.

And then, as long last, the combination paused at Ojinaga, Texas, on the Rio Grande, or Ojinaga, Mexico, on the Rio Bravo, depending on which side of the border you were asking.

Longarm had been ready to get off for the better part of an hour. He tossed his saddle ahead of them and hit

166

the ballast running with his Winchester '73 a furlong short of the sun-silvered open platform meant for passengers and freight. There was a loading chute and pole corral betwixt him and that mail car he'd dropped from as their combination of rail and freight cars hissed to a stop with the engine's tender even with a far-off water tower.

There were half a dozen listless cowponies and a Spanish saddle mule in the corral as Longarm circled the far side. A figure in army blue and another wearing the tall hat and white shirt of the Texas Rangers met him in the shade of some cottonwoods on that side. He knew they'd had plenty of time to get together and compare notes as they waited for him. As they shook all around, the army man told him there were other M.P.s covering the platform from all around, with instructions to aim at anybody he did. The ranger allowed he was there alone. The Texas Rangers were like that. But he was the one who asked Longarm what might happen next.

Longarm dropped his saddle to the dusty ground and pointed with his now unshaven jaw at that loading chute across the corral to explain, "I'm expecting that army bay I wired you all about to get off yonder train by way of yonder chute. I'll be surprised if the she-male passenger who paid its fare from Colorado means to ride off on it alone. But if she does, I mean to let her and just tag along, discreet. We don't want her or even that horse as much as we want the gang of horse thieves she and at least two other wicked ladies have been riding with."

So they waited, then waited some more, and then the engineer was tolling the all-aboard and nothing had happened.

The ranger laconically observed the train would stop next just this side of Laredo after swinging wide of the unsettled Big Bend. But Longarm was running around the far side of the corral before the local lawman finished his gloomy observation and it was still a close call.

The train would have left before he got there if Longarm hadn't fired three rapid shots in the air as he ran. The conductor recognized the customary distress signal and held the train until Longarm could catch up with him, standing on the steps of the caboose with a bemused smile.

He wasn't the same conductor Longarm had talked to back in Pueblo, of course. So they had to start all over. But once he understood what Longarm was asking about he nodded and said, "I recall that Spanish lady getting off just before dawn with a big bay show horse, a side saddle, and a saratoga. They got off at Roswell, hours ago, what made you think they'd be getting off here at Ojinaga?"

"Lucky guess." Longarm sighed. "I'm sorry I pestered you for nothing, and how long is it going to take me to get back up the track to Roswell?"

The conductor told him he'd be lucky to make it by the wee small hours. Longarm thanked him anyhow. He had to thank the ranger and those army men as well. He had no choice. It wasn't their fault he'd outsmarted himself.

So at least he had time for a shave and a shower along with a hearty supper as he waited in a shitty little border town for a train taking him the other way. He knew he wouldn't be there long enough for a serious romance, so he only tipped the flirty Mex waitress an extra dime and left her pure as he found her.

Feeling less call for discretion while headed the other way, when that combination heading up the Pecos Valley finally got in just after dark, he boarded it openly, tossing his saddle and possibles ahead of him to mount the steps of a passenger section smoker. When a colored porter came out to ask him if he'd like to check his baggage Longarm handed him another dime and said, "I'm getting off just south of Roswell, at a run. I'm the law. They ain't expecting me in Roswell and I don't want them to before I get a handle on what I've been missing."

For a dime, the porter felt no call to argue. So Longarm braced his loaded saddle on his left hip, shifting his holster a tad forward to ride both easier, and opened the smoker door with his gun hand to head on in. Smoker cars got their handle, and a heap of business, by not posting the NO SMOKING signs you saw up forward where women, children, and those few men who neither smoked nor chewed preferred to inhale coal smoke and ballast dust alone.

The smoker wasn't too crowded that evening, but the air was already hazy and blue with the windows just shut against the desert cool to come. As he made his way back toward the far bulkhead he preferred to have his back against whilst riding, a familiar figure rose from the very seat he'd had in mind.

"Longarm! What are you doing down this way?" asked the segundo of the S Bar P, Sandy Bowmore.

Longarm pleasantly replied, "I was just about to ask you the same question," and then, not having been born the day before, he'd let go his McClellan to grab for his .44–40 at the same time Bowmore's hand struck his gun grips with the speed of a pissed-off diamondback!

Nobody could have swung a gun muzzle out and up faster. But Longarm fired without raising his own quite so high. Bowmore still got off one shot, but he only blew some stuffing out of the green plush seat-back just to Longarm's left, adding considerable smoke to the already smoky atmosphere.

Then Bowmore had slid down the hardwood bulkhead, slicking the same with blood, to wind up mostly on the deck with his now-hatless head and shoulders propped up against the bulkhead.

Longarm kicked Bowmore's six-gun under a seat and hunkered down beside him to observe, "They say confession is good for the soul and time off for good behavior. So what would you like to tell me about all this bullshit?"

"Go fuck yourself," Sandy Bowmore suggested in an injured tone as the lawman who'd shot him gingerly unbuttoned the front of his shirt.

He saw the segundo was hit bad, through the liver, and doubtless, the paunch. The stomache acids should have been burning like hell if he'd been able to feel anything that far down. So there went the spine, as well. He said, "Let me guess. A man playing second fiddle to a widow woman raising horses for top dollar gets to feeling left out. So he goes into business with another resentful underling, such as her baby brother. Did you have him killed because you were afraid he'd spill some beans in exchange for less time on the rock pile?"

The dying two-face croaked, "A lot you know! Ed Lockwood got caught the second or third time he stole a horse for MacLeod. I warned old Hoss I'd fired the kid as a worthless lay-about."

"He might have cramped your style, laying about the S Bar P all the time his sister was down in Manitou Springs with the W.C.T.U." Longarm observed, not unkindly.

Sandy Bowmore didn't answer. He wasn't ever going to say another word. By that time the conductor and two railroad dicks were standing over Longarm with their own guns drawn but aimed polite. They put them away after Longarm explained who he was and what he'd just wrought. The old and important conductor said he'd be proud to help the U.S. Government in the disposal of the remains or any other chores.

Railroad conductors had such powers. They punched the tickets personal because the railroad wanted someone they could trust riding herd on their cash flow. Conductors didn't care whether passengers took them serious or not. Everyone else on the train, from the baggage porters to the engineer up front, had to do exactly what the conductor told them. For he, not the glamorous engineer, was in command.

So they put the late Alexander Bowmore on ice up forward and let Longarm catch forty winks in yet another Pullman compartment as they rolled up the line through the night. Then they woke him up in plenty of time. Roswell, New Mexico Territory, lay dark and silent under the starry sky, save for puddles of lamplight hither and yon, as Longarm hit the dirt running to let the train roll on a quarter mile and hiss to its stop at another open platform.

Longarm left his McClellan on the railroad ballast beside the tracks as he hung on to his Winchester, moving in quiet. Up ahead, they were dropping off and picking up some mailbags. But no freight was moving either way and only two figures stood on the lamplit platform where passengers got on or off. They weren't moving to get on. So they had to be waiting for someone to get off. One was a tall lanky man, wearing batwing chaps and a brace of Walker Colt Conversions under a tall-crowned dove-gray Stetson. The other seemed a lady of the Mex persuasion. She wore no hat atop her long black tresses and her tawny shoulders were bare above her frilly cotton blouse despite the chill of a mighty late desert night. Her skirts were red and black fandango, but he saw she had on silver-spurred riding boots.

Longarm crabbed to his right to avoid the lamplight as he moved in on them. He'd made it within earshot when that Mex gal remarked in a surprisingly familiar tone, "I wonder what could be keeping him. He wired us he'd be aboard this train, damn it."

Longarm trained the muzzle of his Winchester '73 ahead of him as he calmly informed them, "He was. He just made a mighty stupid move and now he's dead. So don't neither of you move stupid and we'll soon have this sorted out."

They both whirled to face him. The tall galoot in the tall hat froze, considered, and slowly raised his empty hands. The gal started to reach under her fandango skirt, saw she'd never make it, and contented herself with shrilling, "Who told you, you double-dealing bastard?"

One of the railroad dicks on Longarm's side moved in on them from the far side to disarm them as Longarm covered them, saying, "Let's be fair, now, ma'am. If you'll think back it was your grand notion to double-deal me, at the Parthenon, in one of your other incarnations. I bought your gold bricks and helped you put Hoss MacLeod out of business so's you and your pals could sell stock in great demand to the Mexican Remount Service. You can tell me along the way to Denver just who Sandy Bowmore was in old Mexico to see, yesterday. That army bay you got off with here will keep, wherever he's hidden, until you get around to telling us where you have such stock as you ain't unloaded yet."

She told him to fuck himself. He chuckled and replied, "That ain't as kindly an offer as you made the last time we met. But since neither pleasure is possible I'll consider the thought behind the offer and I reckon we all want to get aboard that train, now."

They didn't seem to want to go back to Denver with him. But his new pal, the railroad dick, herded them one way along the platform whilst he ran back to recover his saddle. So they were soon on their way, with the body of their leader and the two higher-ups in his gang cuffed together in a forward compartment.

He'd naturally wired his home office before leaving Ojinaga. And so, even so neither of them had guessed Longarm would meet Bowmore or anybody else before he got to Roswell, he'd primed Billy Vail to expect some answers, with any luck, once he backtracked to where that blonde had got off in the dark with that bay.

So Billy Vail, knowing a thing or two about railroad timetables in his own right, was waiting in Pueblo with Deputies Smiley and Dutch when the combination from Ojinaga rolled in to get busted up.

By this time it was broad day. So as Billy Vail met Longarm and his prisoners on the platform, the first thing he said about the sultry brunette was, "This lady ain't no taffy blonde and she surely ain't no strawberry blonde. So this would be the famous Comanche Rose, with Kansas Red and that other one pretending to be the Widow Penn still at large, right?"

Longarm modestly replied, "Wrong. Allow me to present all three of them, wrapped up, as you can plainly see, in one mighty shapely but awesomely treacherous package! They were hoping to kill me before I could remark on a blonde, a brunette, and a redhead having the same features under the hair rinse and stage makeup."

Chapter 20

Billy Vail stared thoughtfully at the defiant prisoner in the off-shoulder blouse and fandango skirt as he said, "I can see she ain't as naturally dusky as that stuff she's rubbed on makes her look. How did she work them freckles when she was a strawberry blonde? The same tan greasepaint, applied with a match stem?"

Longarm replied, "I reckon. I asked on the way up here, but I can't get her to say a word, and all she'll say sounds rude."

Vail nodded at the sulky gal to say, "You ain't helping your case by carrying on like a first-time offender, ma'am. What's your name?"

She spat, "Fuck you!"

So the marshal shrugged and turned to the other prisoner cuffed to the spitesome little thing. But before he could ask, she jerked the chain linking their wrists to snap, "Don't tell them shit. They're not out to make it easier on us. They're out to make it easier for them, and like Sandy said, they can't prove anything they don't know!"

Vail was too old a hand to let on she'd just verified who their leader had been. He turned to Longarm to ask,

"Don't you reckon we ought to see about connections north to Denver?"

Longarm shook his head and said, "They're all yours, but I have me some other fish to fry. I promised Miss Alvina I'd drop by her place in Manitou Springs on my way back to Denver."

Vail snorted in disgust and said, "Not on duty out of this child's office you won't, you romantic goldbricker!"

Longarm protested, "You sure have a dirty mind. I just wired you Sandy Bowmore, her segundo on the S Bar P, was up to his ears in hot horseflesh, and he was the sneak who hired and fired and ran the whole shebang when she wasn't about!"

He indicated his two sullen prisoners as he added, "I can't get a polite word out of either but they must have that one army bay and as likely some others hidden a short ride from Roswell. I asked if the two ponies I noticed tethered near the rail stop there might be their own. But you can guess what she said."

Vail said, "We can wire the undersheriff in Roswell about them and let him impound them if they're still standing there."

He fished out his watch, nodded to himself, and told Deputy Smiley, hovering nearby with his sidekick, Dutch, "We got us a few minutes here in Pueblo. But not too many. So why don't you boys frog march these prisoners over to that other platform whilst Custis and me send us some wires and pick up some smokes and chocolate bars for later."

As he nudged Longarm to follow him, Vail softly ordered Smiley to be gentle with the prisoners, as mean as they might sass him. He added in a poker-faced manner, "We can wait until we get them up to Denver to take their statements. You boys know what we want them to tell us, but I'm sure they'll tell us in their own good time."

Dutch quietly asked, "Don't you reckon they'd feel more comfortable if we were to ask the conductor for separate private compartments?"

Vail allowed that sounded like a grand notion. As he and his senior deputy headed into the station Longarm soberly remarked, "Far be it from me to tell you how to question suspects, Boss. But ain't the two of us sworn to uphold the Constitution and the Bill of Rights?"

Vail soberly replied, "We are, and I'll thank you to remember I just told Smiley and Dutch I'm in no hurry to press them for details before we get to Denver. So do you see *me* questioning anybody, constitutional or any other way?"

Longarm could only mutter, "I follow your drift." as they went on in, through the waiting room, and out the far side to the Western Union across the way.

At the Western Union across the way, Vail and Longarm put their heads together, composing as short a wire at a nickel a word that might inspire the law down Roswell way to figure out who needed rounding up, and then just do so. Longarm pointed out and Vail agreed that Roswell and all those other cow towns along the Pecos were modest in size and recently settled. So whether those three gals in one had moved in recent as a blonde, a brunette, or a redhead, more honest folk down Roswell way would have noticed. But as they stopped at the newsstand on their way to rejoin the others, Vail made Longarm go over the table of organization as he had it figured, so far.

As Vail coped with purchasing the smokes and snacks Longarm told him, "The Widow Penn was and still is innocent of anything but being a tad sot in her ways. Her kid brother, Edward, found her too tough a boss to work for and unwilling to pay his way through college once he'd dropped out to play perennial sophomore. I'm still working on whether he was led down the primrose path by horse thieves he met up with at his sister's stud spread or just fell into stealing because he felt it had working for a living beat. Either way, we can likely write him off as only a tad more guilty than his sister."

"Then how come he was fencing stolen horseflesh with Hoss MacLeod, the same as Sandy Bowmore?" Vail demanded.

Longarm said, "I doubt Hoss MacLeod ever knew the respected foreman of an honest breeder and trainer was in on it. As Hoss MacLeod told me, truthful, it would seem, he thought he was dealing with Kansas Red, a freckle-faced strawberry blonde leading her own gang. I'm still working on the small fry. Sticking to the bigger fish and one sucker called Ed Lockwood, all of them were dealing with Hoss MacLeod because Hoss MacLeod was the fence you dealt with if you had stolen stock for sale and wanted him to take it right off your damned hands and give you some damned money. As we know, or feel safe to assume, MacLeod had a steady, ready market for good cavalry mounts. As a respected figure in horse trading circles, the two-faced Sandy Bowmore was in a grand position to ask about military remudas without anybody wondering why. I thought that mysterious Comanche Rose would be dealing with the Mexican Remount Service, once she'd stolen the stock as Kansas Red. But since Bowmore and me surprised the hell out of one another on that train back from that out-of-the-way border town, he must have been down yonder explaining how come they'd be dealing with him instead of Hoss MacLeod from now on. So with any luck we may recover more of that stolen military stock than expected, still hid somewheres this side of the border."

"Like Roswell." Vail nodded, motioning Longarm to move on with him as he asked, "Why do you suspect they framed Edward Lockwood with that stolen palomino? Why didn't he just disappear if he was in their way?"

Longarm said, "He wasn't in their way and they never framed him. He was just a shiftless petty crook who operated and got caught on his own. The horses they were stealing, the fence they were forced to sell them through, and the swell market south of the border they wanted all to themselves was what they were interested in!"

They found their way to the platform where their northbound combination was about set to ring its boarding bell. As they strode on to the passenger section, Longarm explained, "Like I said, loose ends, but that blonde, brunette, redhead we're taking in under two names, at least, was a whirling caution when it came to acting. So I suspect it was her notion, when Miss Alvina's brother was caught with that palomino, to come to me as Miss Alvina with that cock-and-bull tale that led us all to the surprise party at that Kiowa Livery. There's no need to go back over the way that turned out. Suffice it to say we put their rival, Hoss MacLeod, out of business, leaving them free to pick up the pieces. I suspect she was scouting horses to steal as Kansas Red and recruiting knock-around help, cheap, as the sulty Comanche Rose. We'll soon find out who she said she was in that Mex fandango outfit."

Vail nodded and decided, "The sweet young thing wanted you killed because you were the only one on our side who'd spent enough intimate time with her to see through all those disguises."

Then he asked with a dirty grin, "So tell me, just how intimate did you manage to get with the sass during her incarnation as the Widow Penn?"

Longarm laughed lightly and said, "Not as intimate as she invited, but whether you believe it or not, there are times a man should quit whilst he's ahead. I hadn't

178

commenced to suspect her, yet, but she may have suspected I had when I spurned her kind offer. In any case, she told her true love it might be a grand notion to make sure I never laid eyes on her again and you know how that turned out."

Vail chuckled fondly and remarked, "I do indeed. Had they just left you the hell alone they might have gotten away with it. I wasn't fixing to send you to Roswell, and you know the State Department frowns on me sending you down Mexico way, you bull in a china shop!"

As they boarded their car they were met on the platform by Deputy Smiley. The morose-looking breed seemed more morose than usual as he told Vail, "Dutch didn't mean no harm, Boss. The gal's all right. She was with me when Dutch took that jasper into another compartment. I warned Dutch to take it easy and I told the jasper not to sass him. But then, to hear Dutch tell, the poor misbegotten asshole called Dutch a son of a bitch and you know how fond of his mama old Dutch is!"

Vail sighed, "Oh, shit, where is he hit and have you called for a doctor yet?"

Smiley soothed, "Dutch never shot him. He just massaged him some with his gun barrel. We got the bleeding stopped and, guess what, the gal I had in another compartment didn't really come with black hair. She had a black wig on over yaller hair. I used it to gag her with when she tore it off and started to scream fit to bust!"

Vail groaned, "Oh, shit, we'd better start with her!"

So they did. To find that, just as he'd said, Deputy Smiley had the spiteful and now mighty odd-looking gal on the floor with her wrists cuffed to leg irons drawn up behind her and what looked like a big black Persian cat trying to claw its way out of her mouth but held in place by some pigging string.

Vail muttered, "Well, she was going to say we all raped her in any case. So she might as well stay that way. Let's go see whether Dutch raped that other one."

Dutch hadn't. They found the shorter, chunkier deputy on top of the prisoner, but fully dressed and seated comfortably in the small of the victim's back. The man he'd pistol-whipped held a bloody bandana to his face with both cuffed hands, whimpering and blubbering like a harpooned walrus.

Dutch looked up to say, cheerfully, "They call him Slats Linklater, but his real name's Hamish. He didn't want to own up to that at first. He says that bitch on wheels in the next compartment would be a Martha Bennet if she ever held still long enough to settle on who in the hell she might be. Sandy Bowmore called her Matty, or his little kitty cat, whenever he could calm her down that much. Bowmore was their ringleader. So she had to be nicer to him. As you likely noticed, before, she had everyone else in the gang henpecked worse than had she been married up with them."

Longarm smiled thinly and said, "Separating the two of 'em was a smart move. With Bowmore dead and her forced to shut up for a spell, we may get others to help us with the loose ends."

Dutch patted the heaving shoulders of his victim in a calming way to say, "We were just talking about that. Sulky Jack Sullivan was the only one we could have nailed for killing Edward Lockwood and you already killed him, so what the hell, and with time off for copping a plea and never calling another lawman a son of a bitch, this little darling may get out by the turn of the century. He says he has four serious horse thieves and some Mex stable hands for us in Roswell. He doubts any of them will put up much of a fight."

Longarm addressed the man Dutch was sitting on to demand, "How many head of military mounts do you have for us and what about other riders off the S Bar P?"

180

The moaning wreckage blew bloody bubbles into the soggy bandana.

Dutch said, "We already talked about that. They have twenty-seven cavalry mounts and four army mules corraled under a sunflower windmill to the west of the tracks about three miles north of Roswell. He says Sandy Bowmore fired Ed Lockwood just for talking about easy money in the bunkhouse. Bowmore was busting a gut trying to present himself as the faithful segundo of a paid up member of the Women's Christian Temperance Union, see?"

Longarm laughed and Vail said he did. Then he told Dutch to get off the poor jasper and fetch some ice and fresh towels from the dining car for Pete's sake.

As Dutch left the compartment, their combination left Pueblo. Leaving his junior deputies to tidy up after the messes they'd made, Vail led Longarm to the club car, where they could compare notes seated with ice cold beer and no dirty looks about Vail's awesome cigars or Longarm's three-for-a-nickel cheroots.

As they made good time north, Vail idly suggested, "We'd best tell the prosecutor's office they'd better keep those former confederates separate before they go before the judge. How do you reckon she managed to get Slats Linklater so henpecked if she was sleeping with Bowmore?"

Longarm sighed and said, "Practice. Some gals are just born bossy and learn early on to pitch their voices in the tones of the mamas who made us wash for supper and the schoolmarms who made us dot our I's and cross our T's. They can wind up cracking their whips over most men the way a lion tamer handles other bigger and stronger brutes. We all do a lot of dumb things by instinct without thinking."

Billy Vail, having been married a spell, changed the subject. So they'd considered other pieces of the puzzle and had the case pictured fairly well by the time they rolled into Colorado Springs.

When Longarm ordered a fresh round of beer as their combination sat out its short stay there, Billy Vail asked if he hadn't said he'd be getting off there to look up a certain lady.

To which Longarm could only reply with a sheepish smile, "I did. I've been *thinking* and, like I said before, sometimes a man should quit whilst he's ahead."

Watch for

LONGARM AND THE SCORPION MURDERS

271ST novel in the exciting LONGARM series
from Jove

Coming in June!

Explore the exciting Old West with one of the men who made it wild!

JAKE LOGAN
TODAY'S HOTTEST ACTION WESTERN!